Ricordi
Things Remembered

Ricordi
is the fifth volume
in the *Prose* Series
published by Guernica Editions.

Ricordi
Things Remembered

An Anthology of Short Stories
Edited by C.D. Minni

Guernica

Copyright © 1989 by Guernica Editions.
All rights reserved.
Typesetting by Composition LHR.

C.D. Minni and Guernica Editions gratefully acknowledge
the financial help of Multiculturalism Canada.

Guernica Editions, P.O. Box 633, Station N.D.G.,
Montréal (Québec), Canada H4A 3R1.

Legal Deposit — First Quarter
Bibliothèque nationale du Québec & National Library of Canada.

Canadian Cataloguing in Publication Data
Main entry under title:
Ricordi: things remembered

(Prose series; 5)
ISBN 0-919349-97-8 (bound). —
ISBN 0-919349-99-4 (pbk.)

1. Short stories, Canadian (English)
2. Canadian fiction (English) — 20th century —
Italian-Canadian authors. 3. Italy — Emigration
and immigration — Literary collections.

PS8323.E4R43 1987   C813'.01'08851   C87-090247-4
PR9197.32.R43 1987

Table of Contents

Introduction, C. Dino Minni   7

Fountain, N.P. Ricci   11

What Can I Offer You?, Dorina Michelutti   41

Like Brother and Sister, Alexandre L. Amprimoz   51

Grandparents: A Fragment, Liliane Welch   59

Peonies Trying to Survive, Marisa De Franceschi   65

Pomegranate Blossoms, Fiorella De Luca Calce   77

The Joke of Eternal Returns, William Anselmi   81

Ed io anche son pittore, Sante A. Viselli   109

For Maria with Love, John Benson   119

Prima Vera, Caterina Edwards   127

The Middle Ground, Genni Donati Gunn   143

Wednesday Morning, Domenico D'Alessandro   155

Changes, C. Dino Minni   171

Antonio, Lisa Carducci   185

Biographical Notes   193

Introduction

This anthology is the first of its kind. It is not a book of short stories by Italian-Canadian writers, which is why many well-known names are missing from these pages, but a book with a theme: the Italian experience in Canada. The title is significant, *Ricordi*: each story springs from something remembered or tries to come to grips with it.

In soliciting materials I stressed that the authors need not be of Italian background or that the stories necessarily deal with immigration. Of the 14 writers represented only eight are first generation Italian Canadians. Most of the others are second or third generation. Liliane Welch was born in Luxembourg, her grandfather a migrant Italian worker. John Benson is a British optometrist, now living in Ontario. What binds all these writers together is a common sensibility as artists, perhaps also the same feeling for roots, identity and memory.

Aficionados of "Italian-Canadian writing" (and I emphasize the quotation marks) will remember *Roman Candles*, edited by Pier Giorgio Di Cicco (Hounslow, 1978), an anthology of 17 poets, and *Italian-Canadian*

Voices, edited by Caroline Di Giovanni (Mosaic, 1984), an overview of prose and poetry. Such readers will look for familiar names; they will find only one: the versatile Alexandre L. Amprimoz.

They will, however, recognize the major theme of Italian-Canadian writing, that of the Journey, in the tradition of the odyssey, in stories by Sante Viselli, William Anselmi, Caterina Edwards and others. They will also discover the recurrent minor themes of the genre, such as the search for roots, race memory, identity, the generation gap and the marginal man. They will notice how these themes have been diluted, even romanticized, by writers one or two generations removed from the immigrant experience.

Who are these writers?

A look at the biographical notes reveals that eleven of the 14 contributors are young, new writers, several publishing their first story. That they draw inspiration from the same well of emotion as the older writers augurs a prolific future for the genre.

How are ethnic writers different?

Canadian writers who have retained aspects of their ethnicity stand off-center in viewpoint from the rest of society. But off-center is a good place for an artist to be. Anyone who owns a camera knows that he or she can make an ordinary picture more interesting, maybe even a work of art, by changing the angle of the camera and the light.

In *Ricordi*, the angle varies with the generations. Liliane Welch's preoccupation with ancestors in "Grandparents: A Fragment" is shared by the narrator in Alexandre Amprimoz' "Brother & Sister". In Caterina Edwards' story "Prima Vera", Maria is rooted to the new land by her newborn child, and in Dorina Michelutti's "What Can I Offer You?" Pieri will have his male power eroded by his

8

child as surely as the mouse nibbled away at his cheese until only the "form" remained. Similarly, in Genni Gunn's story, Rosalba is being "Canadianized" by her small son.

While working on this anthology I had the pleasure of participating, both as organizer and as writer, in the first national Italian-Canadian writers' conference, hosted by the Italian Cultural Centre in Vancouver September 15-19, 1986. The theme of the conference was "writing in transition". During debates on future directions of the genre the 23 writers present expressed both optimism and uncertainty. I had no doubts. In the manuscripts that I found in my mailbox, week after week, I saw the evolution of the genre from the viewpoint of the exile, to that of the immigrant, to that of the Canadian writer of Italian background.

I offer *Ricordi* both as a blueprint and a road map.

C. Dino Minni
Vancouver

N.P. RICCI

Fountain

For the Centennial, the Italians were building a fountain. John Street had been rerouted — not to accommodate the Italians, of course, but for traffic reasons — and a triangle of green had opened up in front of the public library. Tony himself had had the idea one grey Sunday in July when he was hurrying through a fine drizzle to return a book. He was thinking of some design changes he had to make to the front foyer of a hotel complex his father was building for some of the local businessmen when he suddenly noticed, as if for the first time, this tapering green space wedged between the library and the street, the lines still showing between the squares of sod that had been laid there in the spring, and the grass glistening now in the wet.

"It's a waste," Tony thought, stopping to survey the space with an architect's eye. But his mind wouldn't yield up any novel images; all he could think of filling the space up with were the standard park benches, flagstone paths, and flower gardens. He continued staring until he noticed, under an umbrella across the street, a dark-haired girl he didn't recognize peering at him through the drizzle, and smiling. Embarrassed, and realizing that the rain was beginning to seep through his clothes and swell the book in his hand, he turned towards the library.

Before he dropped the book in the after-hours return slot, Tony, protected now by a canopy, glanced down at the cover. The book was an Italian novel his sister Rita had taken out for his mother; it looked like an Italian version of a Harlequin Romance. *Incontro al Paradiso*, the title read, and underneath, *"la tragica storia d'un amore appassionato ma condannato a fallire."* Why was his mother reading this crap? And why was his sister feeding it to her? The bottom half of the cover showed two young lovers gazing into each other's eyes, the man rugged and intense, the woman with eyelids drooping and lips formed into a sinister smile. A white, three-tiered fountain gushed in the background, its outlines obscured by a haze of spray.

Tony looked up from the book to the wedge of green, from the green back to the book. But finally he shook his head. It's just the kind of thing, he thought, that people would expect from Italians. And still shaking his head he dropped the book into the return slot and hurried back through the drizzle to his car.

But over the next few days Tony couldn't get the idea out of his head. Next year was Mersea's centennial, and though it was still only July the town had already been

gearing up for it for some time: a book was being com-
piled, festivities and parades were being planned, hats and
buttons made up, posters printed. The Italians, too, were
looking for a contribution, something commensurate with
their own sense of importance: in a town of twelve thousand residents almost two thousand were Italian, many
among the town's most prosperous citizens.

Every time he passed the library now, Tony would
park his car to survey the little strip of land there, his mind
making little calculations, his inner eye, despite himself,
visualizing what form the thing might take. Once he went
out and made some rough measurements, jotting the fig-
ures down in his notebook. In his office at his parents'
house (where at age 28 he still lived, though as a trained
architect he could easily have supported himself, had his
own place, his own office), his mind wandered from the
plans he was working on for his father, and he found himself doodling little open-winged angels on his drafting
sheets. But when he thought about the idea carefully he
couldn't see how a fountain would reflect the cultural heritage of Mersea's Italians: the only culture they'd known,
past and present, was *agri*culture, and fountains were no
more a part of their lives than they were for the *inglese*.
Tony himself had been born in Italy, and the only fountain he remembered, apart from the village tap where the
women used to go to fill their water jugs, was one he had
glimpsed fleetingly in a square in Naples when a bus had
been taking him and his mother to the port to board a
boat for Canada. For a long time Tony sat at his desk
trying to visualize that fountain, but all he got were the
stereotypical little angels spurting water from their lips and
naked nymphs spurting water from their nipples — images,
he figured, he'd probably picked up from movies and
postcards. He'd never been back to Italy since he'd left it

at age six.

Finally, though, about two weeks after the original inspiration, Tony went to the library to look up some models. A general members' meeting was coming up at the Roma Club the following Sunday (most of Mersea's Italians were members of the Club, and all events of a communal nature — festivals, community projects, Italian classes — were organized through it), and the Mersea Centennial would be a prime item on the agenda. Tony hadn't mentioned his idea to anyone yet, not even his father, who was very busy these days with the hotel project, also planned to be ready for the Centennial, and already running into serious design and budget problems (problems which Tony refused to hold himself responsible for — he'd warned the building's backers when he'd drawn up the original plans, but they'd refused to give in to his suggestions for greater simplicity). But Tony decided that if he was going to put the idea forward at all, he should do it with conviction, and with something solid to show. The more authoritative you sounded, Tony knew from his past dealings with the Club, the less likely anyone would be brave enough to contradict you; but as soon as you showed the least amount of doubt, everyone would be ready to pipe in with their own two lire.

In the cool, sterile hush of the library, Tony sorted awkwardly through catalogues and shelves — he hadn't been in here in years — till he came out with a few books on Italian art and architecture and some tourist books on Rome and Naples and Florence. Back home, Tony almost fell over his mother, who was scrubbing the kitchen floor on hands and knees — Tony never got over seeing this thick-set peasant woman in the gleaming chrome and formica of their modern kitchen, and as he passed by her now he had a sudden image of her stooping to shove twigs and branches under a blackened pot in a fireplace — but he greeted her without breaking his stride, and hurried up to his office.

"*Ma che, te ne vai a l'Italia?*" his mother called after him, but Tony closed the door of his room without responding. She must have seen the covers of one of the books he had under his arm; but when Tony set the books on his desk he saw that the cover which had been showing — the plastic-clad jacket back of one of the art books — had print too small for his mother to have made anything out of it while he passed by her. What his mother must have recognized was the picture on the cover's bottom half, a black and white reproduction of the Mona Lisa. It struck him that his semi-literate mother, who after twenty-two years in Canada spoke almost no English, and who had enough problems getting through a cheap hundred-page Italian novel, could still have made an immediate connection between that enigmatic face and her native country.

Under the fluorescent glare of his desk lamp, Tony began to leaf through the books he'd brought back with him. He looked first through the book on Naples, hoping to find the lost fountain of his youth; but none of the fountains he came across sparked any glimmer of recognition. With this initial disappointment, he began to go through the books more perfunctorily, as if he were going through suppliers' catalogues; sometimes he noted down a page reference for some fountain in a piazza or some frieze or sculpture in a church that might offer a useful image. But it wasn't long before his brain grew numb; everything began to look the same, the swirls and the piping angels and the colonnades, and Tony felt that he must be missing something, that for some reason these much-praised beauties refused to yield up their mysteries to him. He knew little about Italian history and culture — some Roman stuff from high school, some big names like Columbus and Michelangelo and Macchiavelli, maybe a few more specialized ones like Garibaldi and Vittorio Emanuele — but even that little he did know had come down to him mainly through the general haze of hybrid North American culture, and so seemed to have little connection to his Italian roots. The Italy he remembered — and even these scattered memories came to him like dim objects emerging out of a fog — was a village of crude, rock-hewn peasant houses; a ragged, sloping countryside where he tended the sheep and cut the wheat; a crumbling church with a garishly painted plaster madonna whose smiling face showed no knowledge of the fact that the paint on her nose was peeling. His mother, he figured, had probably seen the Mona Lisa on television, which she spent a lot of time watching, though it didn't seem to improve her English much. It was probably fitting, at any rate, that da Vinci's masterpiece was housed, as one of the art books told him, not in Italy but in Paris.

It was only as Tony began to make a few rough sketches, half-heartedly at first but then with growing absorption, that the mist which had settled around his brain began to lift. Now, caught up in his own creation, he began to go back to the pages he had noted and to see the images there in a new light, not as part of some distant culture but as material for his own imagination, to be reworked and remoulded into something personal and unique. When he had a few sketches that satisfied him, he began to make phone calls. A call to Mayor Sterling — whose patronizing good will Tony disliked, but who was a friend of his father's, and one of the backers of the hotel project: yes, the mayor said, if the Italians had some ideas for that strip of land he was sure he could get them access to it (though Tony refused to tell the mayor what his idea was). Then a call to Public Works, about water supply and electricity for the pump, and finally some long distance calls to suppliers, inquiries about marble, about figurines, about other suppliers. By supper time Tony had a pretty good idea of what was possible, as well as a rough estimate of what it would cost.

Tony's father was absent again from the supper table; he often stayed out at the work site now past dark. Meals were getting quieter and quieter these days, Tony had noticed, even though his brother Jimmy was home for the summer from university, and Rita came home every day from her job at the corner store for lunch. What was all this hype about Italian families being so close: Tony couldn't remember the last time he'd hugged his mother, or the last time he'd talked anything but business with his father. More and more it seemed to him like everyone in his family moved in a separate world. At least Rita and his mother had the soap operas in common, his mother keeping Rita informed while Rita's summer job kept her away from the television in the afternoons (though it was a running joke that his mother's plot summaries were more often the product of her imagination than of accurate understanding); and Rita, partly because she had taken lessons through the club, could at least manage a passable Italian. Maybe, Tony thought, there was some kind of renaissance going on with the younger generation, now that it was respectable to be Italian. But Jimmy: Jimmy was another story. Jimmy, who used the house, it seemed to Tony, only to eat, shit, and sleep, could hardly speak to his mother. Even though most of his friends were Italian,

Jimmy had more or less forgotten what little Abruzzese he'd learned as a child, and whenever he spoke to his mother he did so, to Tony's continual irritation, in a fast English that left her helpless and confused. As Tony watched Jimmy wolfing down his supper now, he felt all the resentments of an eldest son rising up in him again: Jimmy, who had it so easy, born in Canada, no problem with language at school, none of the stigma of being a dago or a wop, no black eyes, no bloody lips, by his time Italians had become almost a majority; who'd dressed in blue jeans and sneakers, like all the other kids, worn his hair as long as he'd wanted, played football after school, hadn't had to come home to work for his father or be hired out to some other Italian, to bring in a few extra dollars; who'd got to keep all the money he'd earned on his summer jobs, every cent of it, had always had pocket money for movies and cigarettes and pinball; who'd been allowed to go away to school instead of living at home and commuting. To top it off, and to complete the town's stereotype for the spoiled children of *nouveau riche* Italians, Tony's father had bought Jimmy a new Camaro when he'd gone off to university the previous year. Tony, still driving the battered hand-me-down Ford which had been the only legacy *he'd* received from his father, had said nothing; but inside he had burned with rage.

Still bringing a last forkful of salad to his mouth, Jimmy stood now and pulled his windbreaker off his chair.

"Where are you going?" Tony said roughly.

"Out," Jimmy said, and a minute later Tony heard Jimmy's engine revving up in the drive, then his tires squealing slightly as he drove off down the street.

On Sunday, before the meeting, Tony took a drive along the lakeshore. He was having second thoughts about the fountain idea again, and the drive was his way of trying to talk himself out of it completely. There were many stately homes along the lakeshore highway and in the subdivisions leading off of it which Tony had designed and which his father had built. But most of these were not the ones the Italians lived in — Tony's father was probably the only Italian contractor in town who didn't derive a major portion of his income building the one, two, and sometimes three hundred thousand dollar homes which had become the Italians' trademark in Mersea, and which they scrimped and sacrificed a lifetime for. The design of these houses never ceased to infuriate Tony: the sole criterion, it seemed, was excess, with little allowance made for subtlety, efficiency, or, for that matter, originality. The important thing was that the house look just like every other Italian house, only more expensive, and over the years this competitiveness had set off a dizzying spiral of extravagance. Many of these houses had enough floor space for a soccer field, but it was always boxed up in the same unimaginative ways, huge bedrooms that would never be used because all the children had moved out, expensively furnished living and dining rooms intended only for visits by popes and presidents, useless third bathrooms with long mirrors and bidets and three sinks, kitchens crammed with new microwaves and dishwashers and 30-cubic-foot refrigerators. Then, with the main floor fitted out like a palace, the owners would retreat to the basement, where they had arranged the old stove, the old fridge, the comfortable old couch, the old T.V., and the expensive upstairs would become the refuge of ghosts.

But it was always their homes — homes which seldom

carried mortgages — that Italians pointed to when they wanted to compare themselves to the *inglese*, to pride themselves on their superior industry and ability for self-sacrifice. For the Italians in Mersea, these homes were the visible symbol of having arrived, proof that they could survive and prosper in someone else's country. And regardless of how they made their money — through greenhouse farming, through construction, even through the daily grind of working in the town's canning factory — there were few who did not see their homes as the culmination of their life's efforts. Tony was glad that his father, at least, had not succumbed to this mentality — about ten years before he had bought a modest older home in the center of town, the only excesses of which now were a gilt-edged madonna over the living room couch and a few knick knacks from Florida on the T.V. and on the coffee table.

The lakeshore, though, offered some of the worst examples of Italian extravagance, sticking out like caricatures among the more quietly affluent houses of the *inglese*. Tony drove slowly down the curving highway, looking from side to side and pulling over once in a while to let a honking car pass. Tony had to admit that some of the houses, the ones anyway which weren't laid out in the standard boring ranch style, might almost have attained a certain level of beauty, if the red-tiled roofs hadn't been so red or the glossy white bricks so glossy. But soon all the old excesses began to grate on his nerves again, the little fountains and statues on the huge circular front lawns, the fake stone work, the elaborately arched and pillared entrance-ways. What did any of this have to do with the Italy these people had left behind? Did they get their idea of Italy from the same place as Tony, from television and postcards and guidebooks? Or maybe there was some kind of collective memory operating here, one that went back not just to the Risorgimento or the Renaissance but all the way back to ancient Rome. Even the name of their club, the *Roma* Club, its insignia a picture of Romulus and Remus sucking the teats of a wolf. This was not the Roma of the twentieth century — there were no natives of *that* Rome in Mersea — but of the Coliseum and the Roman Forum. But these reflections, though they seemed to bring Tony to the verge of some insight, didn't settle his mind about the fountain.

The Club building sat at the edge of town just off the main highway, flanked on one side by a funeral home and on the other by the Kinsmen Curling Club. It occupied about five acres of land: a huge parking lot, a shaded picnic area, a bocce court out back, and then the building itself, which looked from a distance like a big barn with a few low stables attached along one side. It had been built some twenty years before, when the Italians couldn't afford much ostentation, and since then it had changed little, retaining both inside and out its almost strictly functional design.

Though Tony arrived fifteen minutes late the meeting showed no signs yet of getting under way. Grey-haired men, their stomachs bulging against weathered black belts and white permapress shirts, sat playing *tre sette* and *briscola* in the smoke-filled members' lounge; a slightly younger crowd milled around in the bar, laughing over bottles of Blue or talking prices and marketing boards and local politics. Tony, file folder containing sketches and estimates under one arm, went around exchanging greetings and pleasantries, inquiring after uncles' families, after cousins' business affairs. There was hardly anyone here who hadn't been a part of Tony's life for as long as he

21

could remember: the weddings, the festivals, the evenings he'd spent at the Club playing blackjack for pennies till three in the morning or working in the kitchen or coat room when it was his father's turn for a tour of volunteer duty. The men here — only recently had the women begun to take an active part in the Club's activities, but they were usually shuffled off into societies and committees, and the Club remained a bastion of Italian patriarchy — the men here treated Tony with the respect and intimacy they accorded a son who had stuck to the fold, with an added deference thrown in because of Tony's university education. Yet more and more Tony found himself fighting a feeling of condescension around them — it often amazed him that these men who had moved so dramatically from rags to riches could sometimes be so simpleminded. He remembered having asked his uncle once about a CO_2 system he'd had installed in his greenhouse: his uncle had had no idea about the principle of oxygen exchange by which the system operated, simply turned the system on and off as he'd been told, investing an almost mystical faith in the wonders of modern technology.

The meeting began about forty-five minutes late. Chairs had been set up in the main hall, with a table at the front for the seven members of the board. Some two hundred and fifty members or so were present, not a bad turnout — almost half the total membership, if you included all the sons who automatically became members at age twenty-one, whether they liked it or not. Tony sat at the back, growing bored and listless while the board went through its business: old minutes, budget reports, date for the annual members' party. Then a report from the committee organizing the three-day Grape Festival in September — the Club's biggest annual event, and a popular one in Mersea, not just among the Italians. But Tony, who had missed the last few meetings, had almost forgotten how unnecessarily tedious they could be: the petty objections, the infighting. There were two factions among the members, divided not as one might expect along tribal lines — Abruzzese on one side for example, and Ciociari on the other — but along lines that were more subtle and difficult to trace. One group, headed by a handful of men whose fathers had come over before the war, in the 20's, had been the first Italians in Mersea. The don of this group was Dino Mancini, a balding, round-faced, round-bellied joker in his early sixties who, having inherited his father's modest pre-war wealth, had done nothing much in his own lifetime to increase it. Dino, despite his slightly pompous attitude towards Italians who had come over after the war, had nonetheless managed, through old loyalties (who had called you over, who had given you your first job) and through a certain easy style of leadership, to attract a fairly large following among the membership. But his main weapon, Tony thought, was laughter: Dino never passed up the chance for a laugh when he had the floor, and in this he seemed to play off a strong Italian need. When Tony thought about the early days in Mersea, when most of the Italians had been united, at least in their poverty, the thing he remembered most was the good cheer, the laughter which bubbled up even when people had no more to celebrate than a shared lunch of bread and wine in the middle of a long day in the fields.

The second faction was headed by a dozen or so members who had come over mainly in the 50's and early 60's and who, while they felt a certain loyalty to the founding fathers of Mersea's Italian community, resented Dino's attempts to use that loyalty for personal benefit. This post-war group seemed genuinely committed to the Club's prosperity (and had never, Tony thought, gotten over their resentment of the fact that Dino had managed to take most of the credit for the Club's founding). But their painstaking seriousness and their attempts to keep everyone happy were often translated by the members as vacillation and under-confidence. So even though they got more done than Dino's group ever did, they didn't maintain the same high profile; and it had more than once turned out, as with the Club's founding, that projects which they had worked and sweated to bring to fruition had with the passage of time eventually been credited to Dino.

It almost always happened that the Club's board was heavily stacked one way or the other, as if these matters were arranged beforehand (and indeed they often were — Dino's group especially would be careful to load the audience with loyal supporters on election day if it had some particular reason for wanting to seize power). But whichever group happened to be in, the other always set itself up as a kind of Royal Opposition, so that no matter could be passed until a good deal of sometimes quite useless dispute and digression had been wasted on it, particularly when Dino was the leader of the opposition, a post he seemed to enjoy, and one he often secured for himself by simply not running for the board in a given year. This year the post-war group held power, and Tony could already envisage from the tone of the meeting so far that he would have a long struggle ahead of him if he tried to get his fountain project passed.

Finally the matter of the Centennial came up. The chairman of the Centennial Committee reported on the committee's plans: processions, floats, fireworks, a folk group from Toronto, a day of contests — elaborate enough to spark a few murmurs of approval from the members. But there was nothing new in all of this, Tony thought, it was like a Grape Festival and a Carnival Party and a Festa de la Madonna rolled into one. It was Dino, though — Dino gave the impression of being a little stupid, but he could come surprisingly quickly to the point when it was to his advantage — who stood up to voice what Tony was thinking.

"We all appreciate that the Committee has been working very hard," he began in his slow, casual English. "But you have to admit that most of this stuff is old hat." Then, having demonstrated his command of English idiom, he switched into a mixture of English and Abruzzese. "I don't say we shouldn't do all these things, I know *l'ingles'* themselves tell me that until the Italians came to Mersea no one here knew how to have a good time. The first time they saw a *fisarmonica* they thought it was one of those things you use to blow on a fire, *come si chiama, 'na mantice.* Dino paused to let a ripple of laughter pass through his audience. "But I think the Italians in Mersea have enough money in their pockets to do something really big. Fifty-five years ago, when my father came here, the lakeshore was all English. Now you only have to drive along there to see what Italians have done. I think we should have some kind of project that people will remember, not just these *fissaroie* that they see every year."

Dino sat down and the president of the board, a dark-haired man in his forties who was a second or third cousin of Tony's, cleared his throat.

"I'm sure no one would disagree with what Dino is saying," he started, speaking, as he always did at these meetings, not in his dialect but in perfect Italian. He had a habit, Tony noticed, of clasping his hands together in front of himself as he spoke, as if he were praying. "And at the last meeting some of the members expressed the same feeling. So if anyone has any suggestions to offer, the board would be happy to hear them."

It seemed Dino had been waiting for this invitation, because now almost immediately, before Tony had had the time to decide whether he should raise his hand, Dino started to speak again, this time without standing.

"There's about three hundred and fifty Italian families in this area," he said. "If we could get each of them to give maybe fifty, a hundred dollars apiece, we'd have more than enough for something really special. If we can't raise the money that way, the Club showed a profit last year, which I haven't heard yet what it's going to do with except buy a few new pots for the kitchen." Another ripple of laughter. "What I had in mind was a little monument or something, the way they have in squares in Italy. I was talking to the mayor the other day and he said there's a little strip of land in front of the library —"

That conniving bastard! The mayor must have told Dino about Tony's call, and now Dino, in typical fashion, was using that information to get in on the ground floor of any idea Tony might have come up with. Tony felt himself blushing with anger, and as he listened to Dino go on, in his vague, rambling way, about the possible form of this proposed monument, he was tempted to simply let Dino dig his own grave — Dino's suggestions made Tony think of the picture he'd seen in one of the guidebooks of the great white monstrosity Mussolini had constructed in Rome to Vittorio Emanuele II: the typical Italian extravagance. But what bothered Tony was that this was exactly the kind of thing the members would go for, and he envisioned the little square in front of the library becoming a running joke with the *inglese*: "And you should see their houses," they would say. "At least," Tony thought, hugging the well-formulated plans under his arm, "if I come forward now I might be able to make Dino look like a fool." So when Dino finished speaking, Tony suppressed his anger, raised his hand, and asked for the floor.

He spoke in English, partly because his Italian, particularly when dealing with technical matters, was a little halting, partly because he knew his English, even though it would go over the heads of some of the members, would give him an extra air of authority; though as he spoke he sensed the irony of having to resort to these defensive manoeuvres to convince the members of an idea which was essentially intended for their benefit. And the English made it difficult to expose Dino's ploy: in any language Tony lacked the frame of mind necessary to play Dino's games, and in English he realized as he talked that even his fairly straightforward attempt to set the record straight — he mentioned his own phone call and suggestion to the mayor — would probably be missed by many of the members. So, even though Tony had arrived with detailed plans, Dino, for the simple reason that he had spoken first, would probably be remembered as the initiator. But Tony could see that any more direct confrontation, which was the only sort he was any good at, and even then he tended to lose his temper, would only backfire on him: had Dino, after all, really taken any credit for suggesting the use of that piece of land? The last thing Tony wanted to be seen as was someone out simply for personal grandeur.

When Tony got to the point where he was holding up sketches, the president asked him to come up to the front to show them around. After the board members had looked them over, nodding and murmuring approvingly,

Dino, sitting in the third row, asked to see. Tony handed them back and Dino stared at them for a moment, then looked up with an indulgent smile.

"Very nice," he said, in English, "but I don't think the English will go for this kind of thing. It's fine to have naked women and things like that in Italy, people are used to looking at them, with water coming out of *lu sesse* and all that. But the English aren't ready for that sort of thing."

So the disputes started. The drawings were handed around, and now that Dino had inserted the wedge his cronies took their shots at hammering it in. Some objected to the cost (which was no higher than what Dino had suggested for *his* monument); others to the idea of a fountain ("The water will freeze in the winter" — just the kind of trite objection that infuriated Tony, and what infuriated him even more was that he had to hedge a bit when he responded to the objection, because he hadn't yet given any thought to the question of winterizing). Someone even suggested they should put up instead statues of the founding fathers, a suggestion which found a good deal of favour, and maybe, Tony thought, the one which Dino had in mind all along. The post-war contingent, meanwhile, from whom Tony might have counted on for support, was left in a state of confusion: to support the fountain would be, in effect, to support Dino's original proposal for a monument, but to go against it would also play into Dino's hand.

The meeting ended inconclusively, and it was decided that the matter be held over for a special vote in three weeks. Before leaving, Tony felt out the board, and found them generally approving. He also spoke privately with the president, to make sure he'd seen through Dino's subterfuge. He had.

In the parking lot, Tony stopped for a moment to speak with his father, who had come in late. His father was looking more and more worn out these days, his hair beginning to thin, the skin on his cheeks sagging; and though his stomach still strained a bit against his shirt, Tony could tell he'd lost a lot of weight in the past few months.

"You never told me anything about this fountain," his father said, speaking in English.

"I wanted to surprise you."

His father grunted.

"Well, if it goes through you'll have to find someone else to build it... I want you to come out and look at that heating system again tomorrow. The way it's set up now the pool in the courtyard will freeze in the winter."

"Look, Dad, I told them a dozen times, you were there, with a glass wall on the north side there's no way you'll be able to keep that courtyard warm in the winter. How many greenhouses do you see in Mersea with glass at the north end? They wanted glass, I gave them glass. They'll have to pay for it."

Tony's father cleared his throat. "Maybe I will too," he said.

"What are you talking about?"

"I put some money into it," his father said heavily.

Tony couldn't believe it.

"What? Are you crazy? How much?"

"A lot."

"How much?"

"Two hundred thousand. So far."

"Jesus Christ, Dad! Didn't I tell you a hundred times that place wouldn't pay for itself? Shit, you've been in the construction business all your life, what got into your head?" Men walking towards their cars were turning their heads, but Tony's temper had gotten the better of him. "Those people are worse than the Italians; at least the Italians don't expect to turn a profit when they throw their money away. I can't believe you'd do something like this without telling me. What do you think I've been breaking my ass for you for the past five years?"

"Calm down, Tony," his father said, his face darkening now. "It's not your money yet."

"Aw, for Christ's sake, Dad, that's not the point."

But now anger and hurt choked him. Inside his car, Tony clenched his fists and pounded them again and again against the steering wheel.

At the next meeting, the fountain project passed, by a narrow margin though not until three hours of discussion had passed, most of it almost verbatim rehash of the objections raised before. Tony had altered the design a little — it had never been his intention, at any rate, to have water shooting out of breasts — but one half-naked figure remained, and she was the subject of heated dispute. Dino himself didn't speak much, but he tried to make it seem — again, by planting an idea here, an idea there, vague enough so he couldn't be pinned down — as if his original idea had been commandeered; but then to allow himself the leeway to fall later on either side, depending on how the matter turned out, he disappeared from the hall, on some pretext, when the time came for a vote.

Tony volunteered himself as coordinator of the project. It was decided that construction would wait till the following spring, to give time to collect funds and get a hold of materials, and to time completion with the official opening of the Centennial celebrations in July. A few weeks later the town council approved the site, and Tony set about making more accurate measurements and plans: he was glad of the distraction; it kept his mind off the hotel. As winter came on, Tony stopped going out to the hotel work site; most of the design problems had been sorted out as best as possible (the glass wall, for instance, had been changed to brick), and now Tony spent his time on some commissions he'd received from other contractors, and on the fountain. The fountain design went through a few more minor changes, quickly approved by the board; and Tony contacted suppliers to have everything ready for spring. But another problem arose when Tony set out to hire a contractor: to be perfectly impartial, Tony accepted bids from all the town's seven construction firms, and — the crowning irony — the lowest bid, undercutting the nearest competition by well over a thousand dollars, came in from a firm run by a German. The board members, unwilling to risk the fallout of hiring a German to build the Italians' fountain, called a general meeting. After a stormy members' session, and then a week of behind-the-scenes negotiating, a consortium made up of the town's three major Italian contractors, Tony's father included, came forward with an offer of free labour; but the whole matter left a bad taste in Tony's mouth.

Finally, in the spring, construction got under way. Pipes and cables were laid, the foundation poured, the recirculating pump installed. A wall of ten-foot high plywood sheets was built up around the work area, ostensibly to protect materials and tools; but Tony guarded access through that wall like a flaming sworded angel, and every evening he came by to put a heavy padlock on the door cut into it. There were more problems, supplies not arriving, marble splitting, intricate cement work crumbling; and the unusually wet spring cut great chunks into available work hours. But all in all work proceeded on schedule and, because of the free labour, well under budget.

Tony himself had refused a fairly generous offer the board had made him for his efforts, but he spent long hours supervising the work. He watched the fountain growing up out of the earth with the spring like something alive, becoming more and more his own, the image in his mind. Sometimes, in the evenings, he stayed long after the workers had gone, carefully inspecting the day's work or running his hand over the contours of freshly hardened concrete like a lover. In the day he often came by to issue instructions or oversee some new addition. He hounded the workers until they began to tease him: "It's not going in your living room," they would say, or, "You're worse than an Italian!" Once, just as one of the workers was putting a finishing cut on a piece of marble, it split in his hands, and Tony lost his temper; but as he railed at the offender Tony noticed the smiles of the other workers and caught himself up, embarrassed suddenly at how personally he had started to take the whole project. Five minutes later, over coffee and cigarettes, they were all laughing together over the incident; but Tony was careful from then on to keep his temper in check. In June the weather cleared up, every day dawning bright and warm; the workers began to put in longer hours, and by the end of the month the bronze head of a smiling young goddess appeared above the ten-foot wall: the crowning touch.

Three days before the unveiling, Tony had the fountain covered with a big canvas tarp. The plywood was taken down, the ground levelled, and sod replaced, and four flagstone paths, one from each side of the triangle and one from the apex, were laid leading up to the fountain. Tony himself looked forward to the unveiling with the excitement of a schoolboy, as if some revelation lay in store for him, too; and when, the night before it, he attended the official opening of his father's hotel (on time but way over budget), he almost found himself taken in by the false optimism of the festivities.

The afternoon of the unveiling threatened rain. But the weather held out through the Centennial Parade, and by three a large crowd had formed around the covered fountain, blocking the traffic coming off of John Street. Tony waited on one of the flagstone paths, making nervous conversation with the photographer from the local paper. There were a lot of faces in the crowd Tony recognized, Italian and otherwise, but also a lot he didn't — a fact which surprised him, since he'd always thought he knew by sight almost everyone in town. Finally the mayor, fresh from his position on the parade's head float and wearing a styrofoam boater with a green, white, and red band, the Centennial's official colours, made his way through the crowd to where Tony was standing — followed, inevitably, by Dino Mancini, who after an unusually vicious election the previous month (too late, Tony thought thankfully, to have affected the fountain) had managed to weasel himself into the Roma Club presidency. They look almost like twins, Tony thought, as each in turn came forward to shake his hand: the same balding round faces, the same benign, indulgent smiles.

After that, under the threat of rain, everything happened very quickly. Mayor Sterling gave a little speech, full of high praise for the Italians; Dino gave a little speech, full of high praise for Mersea — but to Tony the two speeches, rather than building to a crescendo, seemed to cancel each other out, like opposite charges. Then Dino and the mayor, looking in their tight suits like Tweedledee and Tweedledum, each took one end of the canvas tarp and began to pull it back.

"Careful," Tony called out. "Don't let it catch on the statues!"

But in a moment the fountain was revealed: a large round-lipped base of moulded concrete coming up about three feet; then, rising up from a central island, three ascending basins of diminishing size, each of them also moulded out of concrete but lined with white marble. Above the top basin hovered six evenly spaced little bronze angels, wings open, bodies bent forward, and hands holding jugs that were on the point of spilling, waiting only for a source of water. Finally, reigning over all, was the smiling goddess, long hair flowing down her back and a furled toga covering her lower parts but not her breasts. A long round of applause came up from the watching crowd.

But Tony, staring at the fountain as if he too were seeing it for the first time, hardly heard the applause: a horror had suddenly gripped him, and was reaching down now right into his bowels. This was not his fountain, not the one he had fussed and fretted over the past nine months, watched rising up out of the ground. The concrete clashed with the marble, the marble with the bronze: all the extravagances, all the lack of taste — he felt as if some poltergeist had conspired against him and made him build a thing that was the very image of his nightmare.

Maybe the water will help, he thought desperately, and quickly he went around to the little hatch in the fountain's base which hid the filler valve and opened it with his key. He had filled the bottom basin the week before, to test the water system, but after a successful test had drain-ed it again, afraid the water would stagnate before the unveiling. Now, though, he felt the tap giving too easily, and didn't hear a familiar whine from the pipe.

"Shit. No water."

Dino and the mayor had come over now, and Tony, blushing red, looked up at them as he played with the tap.

"Problems?" Dino said.

"Water's off. I'm going to call Public Works."

Before Dino or the mayor could respond, Tony had dashed off towards the library to use the phone there. But the door was locked: closed for the day's festivities. Without looking back towards the fountain, Tony made his way through the crowd on the sidewalk; he'd decided to drive the half mile or so to the Public Works office. Fortunately he had parked about a block away and didn't have to drive through the crowd. But when he got to the office, it too was closed: of course — it was Saturday.

As a last ditch effort, Tony decided to drive out to the Public Works warehouse at the edge of town, where the town kept its machinery and maintenance equipment. Maybe there would be somebody there who could help him. Tony's tires squealed as he pulled out of his parking spot; en route he ran a yellow light and a stop sign, pulling the last stretch twenty miles over the speed limit. The warehouse door was locked, but out back in a work shed Tony found two dirty-overalled men greasing up a small Ford tractor, one an old grey-hair with sagging cheeks and the other a husky, heavily-bearded younger man whose face looked vaguely familiar. Tony explained his problem, and the younger one, collecting up a tool box, agreed to come out and take a look.

A light drizzle had started by the time they got out to the fountain, and much of the crowd had dispersed. Dino and the mayor were nowhere to be seen. The man from Public Works followed Tony to the fountain and tried the tap: still nothing.

"Where's your water come from?" the man asked.

"It's off the library's line."

The bearded man led Tony around the corner of the library to where a metal plate was affixed low down on the library's side wall. Crouching down and hunching his shoulders because of the drizzle, the man pulled an adjustable wrench out of his tool box and began removing the bolts that held the plate. Behind the plate was a large gold valve with a big red handle. The man tried it.

"It's off," he said, the valve groaning as he began to screw it open. Shouldn't be, but it is. Some joker, probably. Must've been last night or this morning, or the library would've been bitching yesterday. Should be a lock on these things."

Some joker. The idea sparked a train of unpleasant associations in Tony, and he suddenly realized why this face had looked familiar.

"You're Doug Vanderhyde," Tony said. "We used to ride the bus together in grade school. Tony Rossi, I lived on the third concession." But Tony felt his voice cracking and his face growing uncontrollably red: the same Doug Vanderhyde who had made life hell for him during his first years in Mersea, with all the senseless cruelty of childhood — elbows in his ribs, spit-smeared fingers in his eyes, the names, the taunts. Tony felt an old hatred rise inside him like a fire, and had to suppress a sudden urge to bring his knee up hard under Doug's chin.

But Doug, just replacing the last bolt, only looked up and smiled.

"Can't say I remember you," he said. Then, rising,

he wiped his hand on his overalls and held it out to Tony. "But glad to meet you again."

Some scattered applause behind Tony's back brought him back to the present with a start, and now he realized he heard, over the drizzle's hiss, the sound of running water. He turned and walked forward until the fountain came into view: the pump must have been on automatic and had kicked in as soon as the bottom basin had started to fill up. A strong, pulsing surge of foamy water was coming up around the feet of the bronze goddess, like laughter, and falling straight down into the second basin; six thick streams were pouring out of the angels' jugs into the second basin; and finally a complete circle of water was falling like curved glass into the third basin. In a moment the third basin would fill and begin spilling its overflow into the fountain's base.

Most of the crowd had gone by now, except for a few who had been wise enough to bring along umbrellas or rain gear. But on the other side of the fountain Tony noticed now, for the first time, his family huddled together on the sidewalk in the drizzle, his mother and his sister stooped shoulder to shoulder under a clear plastic rain poncho, and his father and his brother, one on either side of the women, like guardians, standing with shoulders hunched and arms crossed over their chests. They looked a little pathetic standing there, Tony thought, and the sight both touched and embarrassed him.

"That your fountain?" Tony had momentarily forgotten about Doug, who was standing now at his elbow.

"The Italians built it," Tony said. "I designed it."

"It's beautiful," Doug said. Tony instinctively glanced over at Doug's face to see the sarcasm there, but the face revealed only a pleasant smile.

By now the fountain contained enough water to keep it running smoothly; Tony cut the tap, locked the hatch, then went over to join his family.

"Nice job, Tony," his father said, and Jimmy, speaking in exaggerated Abruzzese: *"Ma che'è success'?* We've been waiting here almost an hour."

That night, Tony could hardly sleep. Just before he got into bed a sudden whiff of rain-water through his open window brought him to the edge of a memory that seemed at any moment ready to burst into clarity, but which refused to yield itself as he pursued it. For several hours he tossed and turned in his bed, kept at the edge of consciousness by the humming rain and chased by the ghost of his memory, Finally, around four in the morning, he suddenly sat bolt upright in his bed: in his mind he saw his own head sticking out a bus window and getting a whiff of some mist blown off a fountain as the bus passed around it. The fountain in Napoli, Tony thought, but already the image was gone, and the fountain was lost to him again.

As the first light of dawn filtered in through his window, Tony rose and dressed, then crept downstairs and got into his car. The sky had cleared and a rim of orange was showing over the trees that lined his street; a coating like glass covered the trees' leaves and the pavement. As Tony drove down the silent Sunday streets towards the library, though, he began to notice little puffs of white, like fallen pieces of cloud, floating idly over the pavement or stuck up against a tree or a fence. The puffs increased, in size and number, as he got closer to the library, until his car was swishing over them as they tried to race away from its currents; they began to thicken now almost into a ground fog, spread out in large patches over the street and sidewalk and bunched up around the corners of buildings. Finally Tony passed the edge of the library and the fountain was in front of him, but all that was showing was the bronze goddess; the rest of the fountain lay buried in a hill of white which had spilled out to cover the triangle of green and was glistening now in the morning's quiet yellow light.

Tony parked his car and sat staring dumbly at the fountain for a long moment. Finally he opened his door and stepped outside. As the white washed around his feet he heard a familiar snap and crackle coming up from it and realized what had happened: someone must have poured a box of laundry soap or something into the fountain, and a night of churning had built up this landscape of foam. Some joker: conspiracy theories began to rise in Tony's head. But then he realized that this train of thought was pointless; the culprits could just as easily have been pranksters like Jimmy and his friends; it was the sort of thing they would do.

Tony leaned against the fender of his car and continued staring, his feet awash in the whispering suds. He could hear the water in the fountain still flowing under the foam, could just see the tip of the jet that bubbled up near the fountain's top. The bronze goddess rising up above the whole scene the way she was, sharp and clear against the morning's blushing sky, made Tony think of a story from his grade nine mythology, a story about a goddess' birth. Venus that was it, the goddess of love, rising up from the foam of the sea. From where Tony stood the goddess' face was turned directly towards him, its lips set in their perpetual smile. What was she trying to tell him? But the more Tony stared, the more her smile seemed to recede into the morning's silence.

DORINA MICHELUTTI

What Can I Offer You?

It is 7 A.M. Saturday morning. Pieri remembers Philomena's birth: she comes through a particularly dense, hair-like mist, first the dark head, then the glassy eyes and finally the slick mouth groping side to side like an eel going upstream. There is no sound. She stays the child like this in his mind for a long time. He sits with his legs astride, forearms leaning on his thighs, hands gripping each other. They finally call him into the delivery room where a blotchy mound of flesh sucks fiercely at Melia's breast. Melia talks, but her southern accent speaks to Pieri of things that are alien to the birth of his child. Words seem to withdraw from her: girl. nurse. tired. shave.

uncertain.; they convey no information. He perceives Melia only as anticipation. Something is expected of him but he doesn't know what. He feels nothing. He stares at the child feeding. A sense of shame builds up in him and he shifts his gaze to his hands which he holds clasped. The muscle between the thumb and forefinger on the right hand twitches slightly as if reacting to an unknown stimulus. This catches and holds his attention. Pieri trusts his hands. And then he hears it: "A child that eats is a child that lives." He recognizes the voice immediately although it is wrapped in Melia's thick accent. He understands. It states things as they are. As they must be. He hears it as a command, even though it is spoken hesitantly, with a catch, as if reacting to the child's hard gums. He knows they are hard. A sudden hammer looms in his imagination and mentally his right hand grasps it. Now he knows what to do. He smiles. Their eyes finally meet and they smile.

It is 7 A.M. Saturday morning. "*Giude Boia*,"[1] Pieri says to Jacu as they walk down the basement stairs to the cantina, "she was born two months ago. It's too long to wait." His hands move before he speaks, then his centre shifts and his body follows. His hands conduct him.

"Don't know anyone whose child has died in all the years I've been here," says Jacu who tomorrow will become Philomena's godfather. "The priests know what they are doing. Problem with you is you don't trust anyone to do a job properly."

Pieri shakes his head, unwilling to argue. He opens the door to the cantina and a waft of musty air pulls them in. The dim light makes shadows of the hanging salami and sausage on the far side. To their right, six shelves hide

---

1 *Giude Boia* literally translated means Judas Hangman.

behind a flowered curtain and hold the round forms of Friulano cheese wedged upright to age properly. They cast overlapping and distorted shadows. The wine barrels are a humped mass on the far right, raised on a platform so that the siphoning process will suck the last drops away from the mother-dregs.

Jacu walks in behind Pieri and even now, after five years, he dutifully utters the opening words: "*Dio Muc*,[2] this is the best cantina in Toronto."

Pieri responds readily: "The secret of a good cantina is humidity. That way everything gets old very slowly. My wine never sours, my salami never goes rancid, my forms of cheese never crack. It takes a lot of fucking work to build a good cantina."

"*Dio Muc*, we Furlans are the best fucking workers there are. Nobody works like we do. Nobody." The ritual complete, Jacu rubs his hands, looking forward to his first glass of wine of the morning.

But Pieri continues as if there were a crowd in the cantina, as if a hundred Jacus were rubbing their hands, expecting wine. "And the humidity has to be constant and natural. No one understands that. That's why their salami goes bad. If everyone was willing to break the concrete under the salami to reach the earth, and then fill the hole with sand so that it could breathe, there would be no problem. No problem. Salami can't be fooled. It knows good humidity, the real kind. Problem is, *Giude Boia*, everyone thinks a hole in the concrete is bad for selling the house. The cake-eaters over here think that if there's a hole in the foundation, the ghosts come in."

Jacu is annoyed. There is no wine glass in his hand,

---

2 *Dio Muc* — 1) God is a German. 2) God is a toad.

his stomach is cold and empty and there is no need for Pieri to go on and on. He nods slyly at the empty shelves for preserves across from where he sits on the stool. "I always wanted to taste that Calabrese salami they put under oil."

There is silence. Pieri mumbles. "Melia didn't have time in the fall. The pregnancy and the factory..."

"Oh well, oh well," says Jacu, "She's a good cook. She cooks polente and muset just like Lisa now."

"What can I offer you, *copari*[3]?" says Pieri quickly.

Jacu shrugs and looks at the cheese. But Pieri picks up a knife from a low table near the wine barrels and unhooks a half-eaten salami from the top row. He pulls the cellophane off carefully and on a grimy cutting board, starts slicing. Usually decisive and given to big gestures, his hands move delicately to make the slices as thin as possible. He takes his time. He puts the knife down, siphons out two glasses of wine and gives one to Jacu. They drink thirstily. Then Pieri goes to the door.

"Melia," he calls. "Bring bread."

There is no answer. In the cantina the two men stare at the floor.

"Melia," he shouts. "Bring bread."

Melia's footsteps finally start down the stairs. Pieri and Jacu look at each other and away, each slightly relieved. Melia comes. Her hair is scattered and she smells of sour milk. Her breasts move unrestrained against her sweater. Jacu makes a point not to look. She glares as she hands her husband four rolls. Philomena starts crying. Melia leaves.

---

3 *Copari* is the appellative describing the bond between men or women when one becomes godfather of the other's child.

Jacu clears his throat and says: "When Leonardo was born ten years ago, well, *Dio Muc*, I didn't sleep with Lisa for six months."

"Go on, go on," says Pieri, turning slightly red.

"True," says Jacu. "True like God is true. And it doesn't stop there. Lisa is learning how to drive."

"*Giude Boia*, you're not letting her drive your car!" He stops stuffing salami into the rolls and stares.

Jacu shrugs. "I haven't got time to bring Leonardo to karate lessons. I keep telling you *copari*, things are different in Canada. You change and you don't even know it."

"No way. Not me. You give your son everything he wants and he doesn't even like your salami."

"Don't talk, *Dio Muc*, don't talk. You build a house before you find a woman and then you're almost too old so you marry a Calabrese. And this is your first child. Don't talk. Just wait until she refuses to eat your precious cheese and opens cans for supper."

"No fucking way!" Pieri raises his voice. He siphons out another glass and gulps it down. His massive hands bend the opaque plastic glass in half and it cracks.

Jacu shakes his head. "Pieri, we emigrated so our children would never know hunger. You can't expect everything else to remain the same. You can't expect them to understand about the eels."

Pieri sighs. "It seems impossible." He hands Jacu a stuffed roll. They eat. He siphons out two more glasses and sits on the stool in front of his friend. This time, Pieri feels it is up to him. He starts: "It was June."

"June the 18th," Jacu replies readily, wiping his mouth on the back of his hand.

"It was June the 18th, just about the end of the war.

We were young.

Only 16. The only men left. Except for the old ones and they don't count.

No they don't.

The Germans, those *Mucs*, took all our grain.

And our fowl.

Even our seed. Even the females and males for seed.

We hid what we could underground, under beds. They would have shot us dead.

They rounded us up as they went.

Volunteers they called us.

In their clothes. In that filthy uniform.

There was me, you, Tite, Ross, Nason and Beppi from our village.

That's all that was left.

We marched with no food in our bellies. We fell.

But the guns made us rise.

We were smart. We were sly. We slipped into a thicket.

They would have shot us on the spot.

Then we realized we couldn't go home.

And we cried.

If it wasn't for the woman in the first longhouse.

That saintly woman.

She said: Children, I have no food.

By her eyes we knew she had no food.

But eat this herb and drink water. Take the clothes of my man. Go into the woods and come back in a week.

We kept moving. From Tisane to Rivignan to La Crosare. As if we were going home.

And the hunger. We stopped by the river Stele in the Baron's woods.

That bastard. Right in his woods.

Then Jacu, you saw them. Black specks. Eels. It was

teeming with eels.

But we didn't have a trident.

We lay on our backs and cried. We should have gone to Germany! Two extra months and no food. Then, Jacu, you shouted.

Right over the Stele ran four electric lines. Quickly. We cut one down. Quickly.

Just one. It fell in the water and sizzled and jumped. And the eels rose all twisted and dead.

Twisted like a string in a pocket.

Hurry. We said. Hurry.

We filled two *Muc* trousers and two *Muc* shirts. We took a chance and dragged them all the way home.

At night. Like thieves. We didn't dare stay.

Then we went back to the woman and brought her eels and a little seed.

She hid us for two months. She saved our lives. That saintly woman." Pieri concludes and sighs.

Pieri remembers her: bone dry and strong. Heavy black skirts down to the wooden shoes. Hair that won't stay up in a bun. It's floury, she says, exasperated, tucking the stray wisps in. She tucks her children in like that. She has four of her own and there are others. They all walk with their heads tilted to one side as if listening for her voice. After the smallest chore they return to her. To her black skirts. Children, she says. Children. Her voice is a reservoir. Pieri cannot see her features. He cannot look at her sadness. He would be overwhelmed by a profond sense of shame. Instead, he looks at the ground and says: "Siore Filumine, I have brought my father's hammer. What can I do for you?" and she replies: "Fix the chicken coop. Take it apart and straighten the nails," she says. "Fix the pig-sty, children. There are no chickens. There are no pigs.''

Jacu sighs. Pieri and Jacu look at each other and sigh.

''Well *copari*,'' says Pieri. ''It's over five years since we built this cantina. Back then I bought 20 forms of Friulano cheese, remember? I aged them, you know my special way of marinating them in wine dregs? Well, I've saved one for the baptism of my first child.

''I still rub them with oil and pepper. Like our fathers taught us. You think everything that woman said is gospel.'' But Jacu is honoured to be the first to taste the cheese.

Pieri shakes his head. ''This is the last form. It will be the best cheese you will ever taste. Better than Parmigiano or Pecorino. Too bad we don't have any polente, but we'll have that tomorrow and the cheese will be better because it breathes in the night.'' He scrapes the salami skins from the cutting board and makes it ready. He pulls out a heavy knife and passes a cloth over it. As he works, he says, ''Jacu, her way is better. She was right. Less work than the messy oil and pepper you use. And it lasts longer. If your cantina is humid enough you don't need oil, just put it under the wine-mother for a week and no mould will touch it. Even the mice won't go near it; they hate the acid crust. And it seals beautifully; makes it nice and red. Haven't touched that form for over a year and it still doesn't need cleaning.''

The moment arrives. Pieri throws the cloth over his shoulder. He proceeds ceremoniously to the cheese rack. The form is much smaller than the new ones that have just started the aging process. Pieri bends over and reaches down to the left hand corner while pushing aside the flowered curtain. At the very bottom, the form stands upright like a stone wheel. Pieri's massive hand has no trouble spanning its shrunken width. Expecting weight, his hand and the form fly back into the air as if flung. It stops in mid-air, close to his face. In front of his eyes is a hole the size of a quarter. What he holds is the crust: a red shell, intact but hollow. "*Giude Boia*," he whispers.

At the sight of his face, Jacu cannot contain himself and he bursts out laughing. He laughs so hard he spits and sputters. "A mouse," he howls, high pitched and hysterical. "A little mouse."

Pieri is horrified. He runs to the door and throws it open. "Melia!" he shouts. "Melia!"

Melia comes immediately. "Quiet," she says, "Filumin sleeps."

"Melia," says Pieri, "*Giude Boia*, Melia, look. Look at the cheese I was saving for the baptism of our daughter. Look." He holds out the perfect, grizzled crust and she sees that it is dark and empty inside.

"A mouse," Jacu start sputtering again. "A little mouse."

"Please." Melia is indignant. "You'll wake Filumin."

Jacu calms down. Pieri says, "But what will we offer our guests tomorrow?" There is nothing left. This was the last one. All I had."

"Quiet husband. We have too much. Too much. We have salami and wine and all that pastry in the kitchen upstairs. It will be a feast."

"But no cheese," he almost sobs.

"We'll cut open one of the new forms," Melia says. "Fruilano is good fresh too." For once Pieri's hands remain motionless by his sides. Jacu stares. He never noticed that Pieri's hands almost reach his knees.

49

Da da, Philomena sings. *Da da da*. It is early Sunday morning and she is already dressed in the two-meter-long baptismal robe. Pieri has his new black suit on. He hates dressing up. He hates shirts. And ties. By some vague agreement he wears them only on certain occasions and the tie during the ceremony only.

He stands at the foot of Philomena's crib and leans against the backrest. His hands hang over the edge. She kicks at the fussy gown and waves her arms high as if to get at the matching bonnet. Her clear eyes jump around the room in bursts of intense focus. *Da da*. She is delighted: *da da da*.

Her flesh fascinates him. He often hesitates to touch her with his hands, fearing they will somehow hurt her, that her skin may catch on them and snag as fabric does. He reaches out. He means to adjust her bonnet, but her waving hand meets his and she grabs his little finger. She holds on tightly. She shakes it. Pieri is amazed at her jerky strength. And her voice. Then he laughs a little and says to his daughter: "It's *pa pa*, my little mouse. *Pa pa pa*."

ALEXANDRE L. AMPRIMOZ

Like Brother and Sister

Angelo's father found a job washing dishes in a small Italian restaurant on Eglington Avenue. His mother was not adapting well to Canada. She had been a beautiful lady, but as time passed only her superior air remained. It gave her face a pathetic, desolate expression. Her dark eyes were bloodshot, her hair untidy and her yellow bathrobe — that had seen better days — was heavily stained with wine. On that cold February afternoon he went to kiss her as he did every day when he came home from school.

"Get away from me," she screamed: "You are not my son! You were born in garbage! Your father, he find you at the dump!"

Whoever she was, she was drinking too much. When his father came home she would complain:

"I have a right to some life of my own!"

He usually kept silent. He was a kind but tired man. After a long day at work he would begin by cleaning the house. Even the sour smells and the odour of cigarette ashes almost disappeared for a while. He was a tall, fine-looking man with a little mustache and when he prepared supper — in spite of his tiredness — he looked more like a distinguished butler than an Italian dishwasher. But was he really his father? That evening Angelo asked his question before anyone could take a bite of pasta:

"Is it true that I was born in garbage?"

His father threw over the chair as he got up from the table and began to hit his mother. She managed to get away and lock herself in the bathroom. He came back to the table a little out of breath and said:

"Your mother's crazy, eat your pasta and don't worry."

Collection 97, the elegant Yorkville Avenue boutique, didn't seem the appropriate place to remember his childhood. From garbage to *Cristal de Sevre*: another success story. *You kept thinking back. The way you understood things then. The way you explained them to your grandfather. You kept thinking back, further and further to that village, to the time when you were four. Dead beetles were like coffee beans. Rivers murmured on great occasions, mainly to stop the enemy. War must have been some kind*

*of spice. You never saw it but you heard about it. Almost
as much as oregano and garlic. And when you were ten she
told you.*

"Am I late?"

Rita was smiling at Angelo. She was a beautiful
woman who had been living with him for a few months
now. A little older than himself, she was in her late thirties.
He liked her long black hair, her full breasts and her dark
almond eyes that made him think of Florentine madonnas.

He caught his reflection in a mirror of the boutique.
*"Fat Wop! Fat Wop! We're gonna sit on you!" The
English boys chasing you. The thing you hated most about
school was recess. Dried salty fish — bacalà — you hated
that too. Every Thursday night she soaked it in water and
every Friday she forced you to eat it. Once you got sick and
she had you eat your own vomit. You were jealous of the
goldfish. They were well fed and no one ate them.*

"Thanks for taking the time, Angelo!"

He smiled at Rita. They were going to "the farm." It
was a splendid old brick farmhouse in the Niagara Penin-
sula. Her father, an antique dealer, used the mansion for
storage. Now that he was dead something would have to
be done about that property. On both sides of the road
orchards made Angelo think of dwarf and thick-boned
skeletons. Even here he found the country cold. *Orchards,
yes. Citrus trees, no. When you were sick your grandmother (why did she have to die and leave you with the
other one?) bought lemons by the crate. At four you believed that women smelled like lemons and men like garlic. Was there any other real difference? Lemonade was
good for headaches, toothaches, colds, deafness, cramps,
nausea, and many other illnesses, including yellow fever
and the Hong-Kong flu. The pharmacist in that village*

sold less aspirins than lemons. One in the morning and a
necklace of garlic made you invulnerable like Achilles. But
the shot in the heel came too! She told you where you were
born, the bitch!

"You aren't saying much," Rita lit a *Gauloise* and
smiled at him from somewhere in that comfortable nest of
fur.

"Sometimes I have nothing to say."

"I don't believe that. When you're quiet, you have
too much to say."

In the morning there were always dead beetles lying
on the kitchen floor. She said they came from the neigh-
bours: "Sicilians!" She was better than anyone else! And
when you were two she hit you so hard, your nose bled.
You had thrown a marble against the bedroom mirror
because you wanted to stop the boy in the mirror from
imitating you.

The exploration of the mansion didn't make Angelo
feel any better. A musty odour of old wood hovered in
rooms that seemed to rebuff human intrusion. Yet he was
comfortable with Rita. It was more than that. They had
met at an art gallery and she had talked to him as if he had
been and old friend. From the start she had evoked feelings of consolation and refuge. Rita was now pulling him
by the hand. She spoke quickly and enthusiastically:

"We'll clear all this, hire a decorator, and turn this
warehouse into a summer home!"

Some rooms were filled with dining room tables
covered with old blankets to prevent them from being
scratched by the matching chairs stacked on top, and huge
blackening paintings with ornate frames covered the walls;
other rooms brought back the painful memories of broken
mirrors; yet others had cabinets against each wall and every

shelf held delicate china and crystal. She finally lead him into a large bedroom on the third floor: ·

"Which bed would you like?"

There were three. He laughed. On a marble table, there was a bottle of champagne in a silver ice bucket. Angelo noticed two flute glasses and a wicker picnic basket. He had been so distracted that he hadn't noticed Rita preparing the surprise.

"I'm the one for you Angelo. I'm going to make you forget whatever it is that's troubling you!"

He smiled. After so many years he was beginning to acquire the certitude that someone loved him. Yet he still felt uncomfortable. Despite his professional success, he was an orphan in his own heart. And perhaps she was one also. The memory of her father made him think. His own father, on his death bed, had answered the question:

"You're an educated man. Think about where you're going... Only in the old country do people worry about where you're coming from."

Angelo had walked away from the hospital feeling lost. He thought about the opera his father had taught him to love.

Do you remember that dream? You were lost. All around you there were mountains and tall buildings. Suddenly out of nowhere came Mozart singing "A cenar con teco." The sound of music opened a way out of the labyrinth. You walked in the direction Mozart indicated, without knowing where you were going. And then you were again in the dump where your father had found you. But what father?

She came back up to the room. A bottle of *Armagnac* in one hand, a box of *pralines* in the other.

"You're still keeping a secret from me. Another woman?" she teased.

"I was born in a garbage dump," he heard himself confess for the first time in his life.

Rita looked at him. He had never seen her so upset:

"You've had too much to drink! That's not funny! Who told you about that?"

"About what Rita, I'm telling you the truth! My father found me in a garbage dump!"

"I was born in an alley! My mother wrapped me in old newspapers and left me in a trash can."

They talked all night in the furniture-crowded mansion:

"I must admit," concluded Rita, "My story is clearer than yours. One of my father's clerks found me in the trash can and brought me in. Of course, we're using the words father and mother in a peculiar way."

"Of course. It's a beginning, at least we share a language," he answered.

Not too many people are born in garbage. Few tell their secret to anyone. Let me touch your long white beard, bring me to the great Sunday mass you say for the moon and the stars. Come and take me away invisible Father, teach me to fly. The dump must be beautiful from above.

"Rita."

"Yes."

"Have you ever told anyone?"

"About my 'origins'?"

"Yes."

"Only a few people. And you?"

"I've never told anyone before. But there isn't a day that goes by..."

"I know," she said.

Little by little, Angelo grew to like the mansion. By

spring it was cleared of excess furniture and redecorated. Rita and Angelo entertained many of their old friends who would drive out to visit. They were happy together and Angelo no longer thought about ''his question'' until one day when he overheard one of the guests say:

''... they're so much alike. If I didn't know better I'd say they were brother and sister!''

LILIANE WELCH

Grandparents: A Fragment

Through the years of my childhood my maternal grandmother remained the one unforgettable presence, the
strong country woman ruling over her farm like a medieval
lord. On her fief I first opened my eyes to poetry and to
the land. Early morning walks over her fields made me
explore the centre of the world: the earth still misty, larks
up in the sky, my hand dug into her large working hand
and her voice bringing alive the entire landscape with its
tales.

There was something of the ancient matriarch in her,
who had given her life to the ground, who felt that on her
fief in southern Luxembourg she stood in the right place.

The land had made her what she was. She stepped in time with the seasons and the earth, attached closely to her particular spot by generation upon generation. In many ways she expressed the spirit of that northern place: for her life had the radiance of continuity, she was jealous of its boundaries, things arose and remained in place. Fiercely she held on to her ground to build on it, to preserve it and to create her village enclave.

She led a life of hard labour, ran single-handedly a farm with cattle and vineyards and raised four kids by herself. Clear as diamonds her eyes knew many secrets. She spoke distinctly about the land and the past, paid close attention to details, knew the names and uses of all things, herbs, trees, animals. She read the ground and the sky and saw what was written for her there as a grower. Her land was more alive to her than her husband.

Her husband, my grandfather, assumed a place in my childhood through his absence. He was already dead when, on early mornings, I inspected the fields with my grandmother, but there lay over him an interdict of speech which had all but forever erased his presence from the face of the earth. My grandmother's closeness and surrender to the land banned a man of his ilk from taking roots. With him I stand at the edge of misty origins and face a new world. Only in my late thirties did my mother release to me image-splinters which lit up sparingly the darkness of silence in which her father had been cast.

He was an Italian migratory labourer who broke the continuity of the family history by eloping with my grandmother when she was sixteen. Destroying the local village customs, he took her to live in a small French mining town a short way across the border from her home, and here she bore four children. Eight years later she returned alone to her home territory, took over the family farm and closed her door to his numerous attempts to come live with her. She let her children walk over to France to visit him but she found ways of making it impossible for him to lay hands or eyes on her again after he stabbed her once. When he died alone in France shortly before the Second World War, his body was thrown into the potter's field. No one, not even her children, ever heard why exactly they lived apart or why my grandmother never consented to give him a divorce. When she was ninety-four I talked to my grandmother about Rinaldo. She told me only that he was a no-good vagabond-rogue who had no land, kept a knife under his pillow at night, lived off the surface of things and places, trekking each year south and east, as far as Turkey.

My brother, a sort of genealogy-detective, sees in our grandfather a victim of the northern Europeans' prejudices against the southern Italians: He could not believe in his wife's village and in the lives it contained. He must have hated their hunger for owning the land and their suffocating life of repetitions. His restless, unsettled life, his brief relationships were reactions called forth by the northern Europeans' obsession for permanence.

When I explore the paths of my background I write poems. They attempt to orient me, they search an approach to the familial ground and the haunting presence of that unknown, forever withdrawing southern ancestor. In these poems the homeless grandfather, who moved from place to place, regarding all residence and relationship as temporary, who took things without regard for origin or consequence, comes through as one who experiences the freedom and mystery of the limitless, open-ended roads. He embodies already the new form of life

61

which we live today, his entire existence having spelled out the deterioration and the death of the old order and the durable way of life of my grandmother.

Without knowing whether he formed me as a person or a poet, I go back to his vanishing figure in my poems trying to understand the significance of his absence, wondering whether he acts out a part of my life on the landscapes I traverse. My poems trek over the imaginary stations and dreams of his voyages: I see him oppressed by the long, sunless winters, the brooding northern village lands. I see him reach for another spirit of place or placelessness, the simple and unburdened life of the road. I see him on his yearly journeys, starting in the north without specific destination, wandering south to burnt fields, under a red glaring sky, over rocks turned to ovens. Was he a pilgrim on his yearly travels or was he merely a sightseer of strange lands? What did he hope to find? A life endlessly fresh and forgiving, a light still new? Was there a constancy in his unsettledness? He always returned to the northern place, picking up again his life left behind months before. He always stepped back into the routine: the boredom of hours of labour, mechanically performed, the servitude of the daily journeys to the factories, winter nights spent looking at his atlas, voices from other emigrant Italians in the distance, the visits from his children. I see him itchy and restless all over again, roaming the ruins of ancient civilizations, venturing further into their maze and now and then dreaming the new world. The years wore on as he exhausted one source of adventure after another. Then he finally died, delivered to solitude and loneliness, in that north from which he had fled each year.

Did he hate his wife, the stern and fervent northern woman driven alternately by her hunger for owning the land and by the weight of ancient habits and a heavy past? Walking through Italy and, in my mind through the eastern Mediterranean lands, trying to walk with his feet, I can begin to feel the geography of his departures, his desperate need of the freedom found on open, windy roads. Climbing in the Dolomites each summer with my Italian companions, I scan their behaviour for signs of the secrets of absent Rinaldo, peer into their faces for clues to confirm his identity. I wonder then whether I'm wanting to retrieve a map which I lost, never had and to which only my poems can give presence? Whether my poetic improvisations are for me the only way through which his absence can reach the solitary walker in me, that walker who longs to be renewed in facing the wilderness?

Sometimes hanging from the rope on a Dolomite cliff I see a lonesome speck moving on a path far below. The sun beats on my back. As I hoist myself over the last ledge of the wall to the peak, I think of Rinaldo's flights south each spring. His migrations speak against the blurred and blurring, impoverished everyday existence and call me away from it into a risk, out of the routine-bound flat life into the glow of human longing, out of myself into climbing real mountains, climbing word-mountains.

My awakening to my grandparents' plights and adventures began when in 1978 I first went regularly to Italy. The old-fashioned ambiance, the hospitality toward foreigners, the firm sense of social relations and family commitments returned me to the world of my childhood. In Perugia, Angelo Chiuchiu, a professor helpful, creative and alive, not only taught me my first lessons in Italian, the ancient, beautiful language which all along had pulsed through my veins, but his very person shone brightly with the thread of the Latin heritage which helped to shape the story of my life.

I have learned from my treks within genealogy that a family epic is something as forbidding, incomprehensible and ritualistic as a wilderness area; that when you are looking for one specific ancestor at the beginning of a path, another one is awaiting you at the next turn. Thus at those moments when I was most intently searching for my grandfather, images of my grandmother spoke to me. I also learned that, whether remembering the web of experiences lived with my grandmother or examining the cast of characters in faded photo albums, unawares I was always penetrating from the outside of my background and antecedents into the inside of my own life's narrative.

MARISA DE FRANCESCHI

Peonies Trying to Survive

There are fewer flowers this year. That's the first thing I notice. Then I feel the guilt.

When she phoned earlier today, I was annoyed, as always. It was eight o'clock, Sunday morning. I went through the usual routine: Why does she always call me! Why does she always have that false sense of urgency in her voice! One week it's ''come and get the fresh asparagus and bring me a few cans of coffee.'' Next weeks it's ''the lettuce and I'm out of detergent.''

Sometimes I mutter my protests to my husband, sometimes to my mother, but usually I just mutter to myself — anger building in me, knowing I am impotent against her. I always obey. And I know that's why she calls me.

I often think she uses the asparagus and the lettuce only as an excuse. What she really wants is to feel the power she has over me.

This thing about food annoys me. I have more important things to do than to run down there to pick up a bunch of asparagus. But she belittles my artistic pursuits, saying if I had grown up like her I wouldn't have had time for such stuff.

Food has always commanded great respect for her. Food was the answer to everything. Depressed? "Eat! You'll feel better." A cold? "Hot milk with honey." Tired and listless? "Boiled barley."

My father always said food was just something you had to ingest in order to sustain the body. A necessary inconvenience. I guess I am of the same opinion. Not her. She is the kind who seems to live for that sort of pleasure of the palate. When she sits down to a meal, she sits down. She lingers over her food, savouring it with all its richness, like a horny old man looking at a delectable young body. Her own body is no such attraction. She is grotesquely overweight these days.

When she was young, she was always hungry, she says. She survived two world wars, and more than half her life has been spent trying to earn enough money to feed herself and her children.

"As long as you have something to eat, clean clothes, and your hair is neat and combed, what else could possibly matter?" she would say.

Maybe, love, I thought.

There aren't any flowers around the pear tree. Usually she digs a doughnut shape of earth around the tree and she plants impatients. I look at the rest of the yard. Things are missing.

I am happy to see she has planted geraniums in her two pots on the front porch. It hasn't come to that yet. And the self-seeded flowers and perennials are there too, though she played no role in their resurrection. They just continue to multiply, will continue to do so even after she is gone.

The lack of her hand shows. The chicken coop is empty, the garden untilled.

The small, red-bricked house is now dwarfed by the spreading pines that once framed her front window, and I think it looks queer to see how they have grown while the house has remained the same. It's a tiny house — one room across the front with a kitchen at one end and a combination living room-dining room at the other. There are two tiny bedrooms and a bathroom. She says it's enough for one, and that's true.

Is she trying to tell the world something with this house? Is she trying to tell the world that she needs no one?

When I was a little girl I used to love going to grandma's. I approached my summers full throttle. Freedom and liberty were at hand! Grandma allowed me to do just about anything whereas my mother never even allowed me to have roller skates or a bicycle.

She let me go to the farm across the road all day long, as long as I popped in for lunch and supper and came to bed when it was dark. The Lalonde's place was a real farm. Hundreds of acres and all sorts of animals plus an assortment of grandchildren that came and went all summer long. Old Mr. Lalonde and his three sons ran the farm. The place was always in a bustle. We collected eggs, wiped them with a damp cloth and placed them in their containers. We cut the lawn and cleaned the farmhouse. Sometimes old Mr. Lalonde would give us apple pie or maybe pumpkin with real cream. Grandma always bought her pies from the breadman. Once I asked her why she didn't make pies like old Mrs. Lalonde and she told me she had never had the luxury of being able to make such things when she was in the old country. Consequently, she had never developed the custom. "Where do you suppose we would get the sugar," she had said. "We had trouble getting enough cornmeal to eat!"

On Sundays my parents came down to see how I was doing. Naturally I looked healthy. Kids generally do in summer after a dreary Canadian winter. And, it must be said, of course, Grandma always fed me well. "Why do you think I grow all this stuff?" she would say. "It's for you and for them" — pointing to my parents — "so that you can eat decent food and not that store bought trash."

I remember one Sunday visit. I had just come home from church. The Lalondes — all of them — always went to church on Sundays and Grandma insisted I go too. She herself never had time for church. My friends and I were playing in the Lalonde yard, over by the shed that Mr. Lalonde was building. I stepped on a plank which had a rather long nail sticking out. My little Sunday sandals hadn't had a chance. I remember how I cried and laughed. It looked weird. It looked as if I had a platform beneath my foot.

Old Mr. Lalonde came out and yanked the plank off and Mrs. Lalonde sat me down in the kitchen and put my foot in hot, salted water. Dark red blood oozed out of my foot and it swirled around in the pail.

As I sat there I saw my parents drive up to Grandma's

across the road and Mrs. Lalonde made me promise to tell my mother so that I could be taken for a tetanus shot. Naturally, I didn't tell her. I could have died, I suppose, but I would rather have died than have to tell her or Grandma about the nail.

I walked as best I could and mother noticed I was walking strangely. I told her I had stubbed my foot on a rock. Grandma jumped in protectively. It wasn't all out of concern for me; it was for herself too. "What are you worried about? A little thing like that! Why don't you look at her face and see how she's filled in! Look at those skinny legs and see how they're fattening up." She and mother never got along.

I didn't see the discord until I was older. Grandma always talked about the wonderful things she used to send my mother and my aunt. Every Christmas and Easter she sent them clothes and once in a while a real toy. "They were the best dressed children in town!" she would say.

"... the only ones without a mother and a father," my mother would say when we talked about her youth. Oh, she would verify it was all true about the gifts, but the tone said something different.

"When did you ever see her?" I asked my mother once. "Very rarely," she had replied. "She went away to work. Our father had gone to America and forgotten about us. So I guess she had no choice. She sent us money and clothes, but we rarely saw her. You couldn't blame her, I suppose. One trip home and she would have used up all her savings."

When her two daughters were old enough to work, she had managed to find them employment in Fiesole — a little town in Tuscany, not far from Florence, which was where Grandma worked. They saw each other a little more then since they were closer, but it was still difficult. With only one day a week free, it was not easy to get to Florence from Fiesole and back.

When the Second World War began, she and my mother and my aunt walked and hopped on trains until they got home.

During the war, that was the only time they actually lived together. Then, mother met father and they left the old country and my aunt met my uncle and did the same. It wasn't your regular family set up and I can see why love is lacking now.

My mother says she's just glad she had a wonderful grandmother who loved her and took care of her all those years. When I hear that, I think about my feelings for Grandma and I try to understand how and why I lost my love for her. I loved her once — as a child. I know I did. I must have. But it is gone. Since one particular incident.

I was about twelve. Mother was working on a tobacco farm that summer and Grandma was with us. I was at that awkward age — a girl growing into a woman. And all the visible signs of womanhood were being cast upon me. This tormented me to no end. Breasts were such a bother. How uncanny that I should grow such vulgar appendages. In a household where things of the body are kept secret, it was a curse to have been given visible proof of growing up. It was an enormous burden for me to have to walk around with little lumps beneath my clothes. Consequently, I always walked around slightly stooped and grandma shouting, ''Stand up straight!'' only made me stoop more.

So, when I wore that loose fitting blouse with the long sleeves to wash the basement stairs, I was only trying to hide my body. How could I explain to Grandma that I was ashamed. I didn't even know it myself. All I knew was that I felt uncomfortable.

She got upset with me for being so foolish. And she was right, of course. It was foolish to try to wash the stairs wearing a shirt with sleeves that dipped into the pail.

She told me to tuck the shirt in and roll up the sleeves for heaven's sake! Didn't I see I was getting soaked! But I wouldn't listen. Naturally, she got angry with me and she told me to just take the shirt off. Then she tugged at me. The thought horrified me and I ran from the house, leaving my work unfinished.

Things have never been the same since.

Perhaps I was too sensitive or she wasn't sensitive enough. After all, she hadn't gone through the perils of having to actually raise her children; her mother had taken up the task for her.

A few years ago she stopped keeping ducks. "Why bother," she had said. "It's just more work and my legs are getting weak and my shoulders hurt." But she still had the chickens and the garden. I could still enjoy the feel of a warm, soft egg reached beneath a trusty hen.

I can still see her walking out to the chicken coop with her bucket of feed, calling to her hens as they came clucking along. She used to say they knew her; they trusted her.

I began to see a pattern. The way she was with her animals, that's how she was with children. She was gay around them. She seemed to sincerely enjoy their presence. She gave to them, as she gave to her animals and to the growing things around her. She gave endlessly, barring no expense, asking only for a kiss in return.

They, being what they are, gave the kiss willingly and with unabashed candor.

Perhaps it is knowledge that kills love. Perhaps it is growing up. I started to see things I had never seen before

and question others I had never questioned before. I started to want to know the truth — as if that would bring anything but sorrow and pain.

With my own son, she is as she used to be with me. I watch
her and I remember. Her old eyes light up and I feel the
guilt. Why can't I love her? What has she ever done to me
that is so unforgivable? Innocence lost, I lost love.

Why can't I remember the good things? The gold
watch she sent me from Montreal when she worked there
as a maid. The play set of table and chairs that came that
Christmas. The typewriter she gave me when I started high
school. All expensive gifts for a grandma who worked on
her hands and knees. She had done the same for her children. Sent them things. Expensive things. Things no one
else had.

The chickens went soon after the ducks. That upset
me. It was the way she did it. She had us go down one
Sunday — mother and I and my aunt — and she had us
slaughter all the hens! Just like we used to in the old days
when we first arrived from the old country. She and my
aunt stuck knives into their skinny throats and then they
held them upside down to drain the blood as they flapped
wildly. One after the other, they slaughtered them. Then
we boiled water, plucked them, bagged them, and prepared them for the freezer. Mother and I could handle that
part.

She was as unattached as a butcher. There was no feeling for the animals she had fed and watered through cold
and dreary days or hot, humid ones — the animals that
were her only companions for days at a time, the animals
that trusted her. When it was over she said, ''Well now.

The three of you can divide them up and take them home. You have enough to last all winter.''

She was practical. She simply couldn't handle the work anymore. Just walking to the chicken coop had become a chore.

The garden went a few years after that. Last year all she had were a few tomatoes and some beans. This year the ground has not been broken.

I guess I knew this would be one of my last times down there. Perhaps she knew it too and perhaps that's why she looked through me as she did. It is a replay. I always feel the anguish as I leave the house. It is only when I am nestled inside my car and a safe distance away that I can actually look her in the eye. Otherwise, I avoid her gaze. And she used to avoid mine too. Lately, however, I've noticed she looks at me with something in her eyes. I would call it innocence if it were in someone else's eyes. I don't know what it is, but she looks at me in such a way and the hurt penetrates. Does she know how I feel?

I wonder if she'll change now that she's near the end.

When her brother died last year, we hated to tell her. We never learn. We always think this one is going to get to her, but it never does. We keep on giving her the benefit of the doubt. Maybe we do it more for ourselves than for her. After all, she is in our blood. When we told her, she just put on that false sorrow of hers which we recognize immediately and we are hurt. The next time we went down, she didn't even mention it.

It was the same when the Lalondes died. It was funny when old Mr. Lalonde was actually younger than Grandma. But when he died she said, ''Oh well, what can you expect at his age.'' She never thought of herself as an old lady; not until recently.

For years she had worked for the Lalondes. I remember her walking across the road to load the milk containers on the milk truck. Old Mrs. Lalonde could never lift such weights.

Work never frightened her. She had worked ever since she could remember. It was by scrubbing other people's floors and washing other people's dirty laundry that she managed to scrimp and save to buy the tiny farm and build this house.

She says she's never had it so good and I suppose she hasn't if you compare it to what she had before. It's just that I would have expected much more. She says we all expect too much these days. But I don't mean that I would expect more in terms of material things; I would expect an emotional more. I couldn't see myself living alone year after year the way she does, without a man.

She was only in her twenties when he left her and as far as I know, she has never had another. I figured she was too old fashioned to get involved with a man while her husband was alive. When he died, Grandma was in her sixties. My father joked about how she could go out and find herself a man. I had taken father's remark seriously. She had just moved out to that desolate little house and I didn't know how she would be able to live there alone. She managed, however. She managed for well over thirty years.

All she ever said was that she didn't need a man. What had he ever done for her! Only leave her with problems.

It seems we stay less and less each time we go. She asks if I want coffee. Usually, I tell her to sit still; I'll put on the pot. These days it's such an ordeal for her to make coffee for more than herself. But this time I tell her I don't want any and she doesn't say much. She just looks around and asks when I'll be down again.

It's as if her body is slowly deteriorating, leaving only an alert brain.

A few weeks back when we all went down, she was so flustered we decided not to do that to her again. She was exasperated with having to open a bottle of beer for my father and my husband. "Get your own glasses," she muttered. "My shoulder hurts when I raise my arm." Then she sat down and said an astonishing thing. Something I never thought I'd hear her say. "I'm tired," she said. "I'm tired of living."

She wasn't speaking to us or to anyone in particular. She just said it, and we understood.

We were all touched by her feelings, but only my father knew how to change the mood. "So you want to die on us, do you! I hope you live to be a hundred," he said, in jest. "That way we'll get all that pension money."

Such statements exasperated my mother. Even though she couldn't feel love for the woman, she still had a sense of decorum.

Grandma said she was planning on living to a hundred just to spite him. And then she amazed us with another unexpected remark. "And don't be so sure you're going to get any of my money," she said. "I've made out a will."

She still had a tidy sum that she insisted upon sharing with us — one of the few things that still gave her some satisfaction. In her mind, as long as she had money, she had power.

She must know she can't buy our love! She must! I guess she does, but she also knows us. She knows we can't refuse her gifts and she also knows that once we have accepted them, we have an unsigned contract that says she can interfere in our lives. She holds us to her the way she held her children when they were young: with materialism — because she knows no other way.

Now Grandma had made out a will. Everyone calmed down and a sort of reverence surrounded her — an aura. We all looked at her inquisitively, asking questions with our eyes. It was as if we were looking at a ghost and we waited for it to speak.

"I made out a will and you'll see it when I'm dead."

My father had tried for years to get her to do just that. She would have no part of it. "As soon as you make out a will, you die," she would say. Reason never helped. When father would tell her that her life savings would be taken by the government, she would say, "I don't care who gets it!" Mother would cringe at such remarks.

I suppose she has had to adapt. She has had few choices. She has had to develop a tough skin. But it's that lack of need, that self-sufficiency that I hate the most.

So, this day, as I pull out of her driveway, I think about the will and I think about how this place will look when she will be gone. And then, as I turn my head to guide the car out, I catch a glimpse of the old Lalonde place across the road and the image remains in my mind all the way home: tall grass that needs cutting, weeds overgrowing the flowers, a broken pillar on the front porch, and peonies trying to survive.

FIORELLA DE LUCA CALCE

Pomegranate Blossoms

A scent of pomegranate blossoms permeated the night. The air was cool. I couldn't help shivering. The shawl barely managed to cover my body and it did little to warm us both. Tenderly I stroked my slightly swollen belly and felt a faint stirring within. Yes, the walk had done us both some good. I had needed to get away and find some peace of mind. I knew I would find it here among the grapevines and the pomegranate trees.

Footsteps approached from behind the thicket. The

leaves rustled as two hands parted the foliage. It was Andrea!

Quickly, I tightened the shawl around my body.

"How did you find me?"

"Your mother said that you had gone to Zia Maria's house. I didn't find you there so I knew she had lied. I knew you would be here."

I cursed him silently for knowing me so well.

"Why have you come back? Before you left for Caserta you said you would never try to see me again."

"So I lied."

"You know what would happen if my parents were to see you with me. God knows what they would do to you. And what about Paolo?"

"Paolo knows that no matter how much you love me you would never cheat on him. Certainly not now that you are married."

The gall of him! "And what makes you so sure that I still love you?"

"Say it to my face then. Come, tell me you don't love me. I'm here now, am I not?"

"I don't love you, Andrea."

"Look at me, and say it!"

I repeated the words, without feeling — like a dummy — detached.

"You're a liar!" I shrank back as he grabbed my arms. "You love me not Paolo. You married him because your father forced you. I wasn't good enough for Cesare Vitale's daughter, was I?"

"Stop; you're hurting me!"

Andrea froze. "*Dio mio*, Katia! I don't know what came over me." He drew me into his arms. Instinctively my arms wound around him.

"Andrea, you must let go of the bitterness. Try to understand. Everyone expected Paolo and me to marry one day; ever since we were children. Paolo is an honest man. He is a good husband."

"But it's me you love; me you should have married. We belong together."

"Andrea —"

"I'll take care of you."

"I'm a married woman, Andrea."

"God, if only you were with child. Then you would belong to me."

I blanched. He couldn't possibly know! He must never know.

"You are a fool."

"Katia, listen to me. We could go away from here. We could be together and no one would care."

"No! You have to stop talking dreams. There's no turning back for us. We have no future." His stubborn expression said that my words had been useless. I had to make him see reason.

"I'm leaving with Paolo the day after tomorrow. We're going to America." I expected him to swear, shout, anything but the intolerable silence that enveloped us.

"So my coming here has been useless," he said, nervously fumbling for a cigarette.

"I'm sorry." I moved to touch him but he turned from me, angrily flicking the cigarette to the ground.

"Damn you, Katia!"

The tears slid down my face and I did nothing to hide them. The scent of the pomegranate blossoms seemed somehow sharper. I pictured them silently falling from their branches.

"I've always loved you, Andrea."

"I know."

"I won't forget you." The life within me moved as if to bind the promise.

"Nor will I, Katia." Gently he pulled me to him. "You and I my love will never be happy."

I placed my hand over his lips. I traced them with my fingers and etched them forever in my thoughts. He brushed his lips softly over my hands.

"Arrivederci, Katia?"

"No. *Addio*, Andrea."

"*Addio*."

I watched him as he walked away from me. I stared long after the darkness swallowed him. The breeze brushed past me carrying its sweet, unforgettable scent.

"You and I my love will never be happy."

Gently I placed my hand over my belly. The life within flowed through me, giving me renewed strength. I would survive.

WILLIAM ANSELMI

The Joke of Eternal Returns

I
Allegretto

> *Ed a una uscita di galleria ti ritrovi in*
> *faccia il sole che ti fruga i pensieri,*
> *legge dentro la nostalgia...*
>
> Claudio Lolli, *Viaggio*.

The tunnel — then the mid-afternoon sun floods the
windows; it glistens on the metal pieces, drawing knotted

designs on the wooden seats. Before the light dissolves the dark, expectations, remembrances, the compartment is jolted right, left, right, left accompanied by a cranked noise. When the eyes adjust themselves to the fragrance of the mobile palette, which, for thirteen kilometers has been haunting the senses inside the railed cave, a call to order is issued by the ghost in the skull. Exactly now, an accented voice bursts through the loudspeaker to announce: "Trigliano, Trigliano Station."

This time what has emerged from the unknown is more varied than the last: two older women, arm in arm, leisurely strolling underneath a black umbrella; on the opposite side of the street, reclined against the brick wall, a peasant in blue overalls, akin to the sky of this afternoon, and the lobster-red torso, sprinkled at its center with gusts of black, silver tufts. Already, while the brain is still snapping postcards, the train has squeezed out of its aisles, labyrinths, entrails, a few sleepy-eyed militaries, commuters, and some German, possibly American tourists. On the platform, two tall blond-haired men, and three girls, one dark-haired, with a transparent white skirt, the other two light-blond in cut-offs, accentuating the curves. Massimo walks out of the station, still considering origins, female origins. The hill is the first thing that confronts him with a somewhat mythicized return. There is the abandoned funicular — the coach is rusting at the base, the blue paint is peeling, and along its sides the nettle, the spike, the ivy are forever growing. One day there will only be a green encasement, and the local children will go and chase the vipers out of it with a pellet gun.

There are four ways to reach the top of the hill from the station: on foot, it is four kilometers if no car succumbs

to the blister-ridden thumb; by taxi, if you are familiar
with being short-changed; by a lazy bus that will spin you
around the many curves bringing you closer to strangers;
and, yes, a steep shortcut of gravel and grass. The top, as
of this afternoon, is not the ultimate goal of our distinguished fellow traveller. Massimo, the Wondering Ulysses,
is to mark a return that, first of all, involves a bath. The
house where he will freshen up is very close to the station.
You walk about a mile, a little more than a kilometer,
with two suitcases weighing approximately sixty pounds,
to what is, by definition, familiar grounds. And time,
never enough time to be aware of the everchanging details,
from what memories have solidified into a pattern in the
marrow.

Footstep after footstep, the eyes darting left, right,
confirm that the bar, Paolo's Bar, is always beside the
church, and that there is a new clock on the traffic island in
the middle of the intersection of the two roads, one leading to Trigliano and its Gothic cathedral, the other to the
super highway that connects Florence to Rome. A bathtub,
a bottle of Trigliano white beside it, the walkman... the
image, fragmented, in Massimo's inner eye. His lips taste
the sweet of a pleasure soon to be realized, and hello? The
girl walks on by, oh seven hundred etc. steps from small
mankind... everybody sleeps the afternoon away. Should
he ring or knock? The key is in the pocket, but the doorbell, isn't it a nipple?

Mr. Pavonazzi's afternoon nap came abruptly to an
end when, at precisely six to the hour, the doorbell rang a
sequence of notes: Verdi's *Va Pensiero*. "I was expecting
you, I was on the phone when..." Massimo, sweaty, without sleep for thirty-six hours, breaks the joke with a banal
Hello, Uncle Joes inside an embrace. Uncle Joes takes

charge of his suitcases and shows him where he will be sleeping. Rooms, keep changing allocation; should you be marking a visit, be sure beforehand to indicate where the roots grew. In this case, the roots, after three years, lie in the room that bounds on the next apartment; not in the one that from the window gives onto cramped blooms: nettle, entwined vines criss-crossing the soft warm air, small apple trees and armies of dandelions — for this room cuts the deep sleep into sudden anxious moments, when the windowpanes rattle like old women's dentures in an earthquake and the emptiness fills up with balloons prick-ed, from the inside, with "fuck the holy virgin wearing blue polkadot underwear" or "oinking hog-god trapped in a coal mine" both heard last at the age of fifteen. The railway tracks are parallel to the super highway, and they are only thirty meters, in a bee-line, from where Massimo will be sleeping.

"How was your trip?" To someone who has never travelled, the question would probably elicit a number of stories, each one separate and yet with an under-running leitmotiv: the individual's responses to the ever-changing, yet static, world; the stories, presumably, would be splut-tered out into some kind of coherent presentation. Mas-simo, who has by now gone back and forth between Canada and Italy for a number of years, which he will never specify, like an aristocrat his right-leaning sympathies, or well-to-do women when asked for their age, rebukes opening the window: "Not bad, the plane was delayed. They told us it was because of engine troubles. It took me a while to find the bus to the station in Rome. There was a strike by au-tonomous drivers, or something like that. Finally, an inde-pendent worker came and told us that the bus to Girondola would be making a stop at the station before three..." He is interrupted by: "So you caught the five to four train?" "No," he replies, "little one", as he is known by his uncle. "I took the local at four-seventeen which skipped two stations and so I arrived there before the Milan express."

"That's wonderful, I knew you would be here before seven, but I wasn't sure because of the strike, so I just waited around." And with that the uncle grabs the suitcases and carries them into the guestroom.

"I am going to take a bath, o.k., Uncle Joes?"

"Sure, if you like it cold. You will notice that the warm water is cold. You know how it is…"

"Don't worry, I will be fast about it." He goes into the bathroom, carrying a pair of white shorts and a bar of soap, while the sun is already dancing from a corner of the bathtub into the series of sparkles alongside the faucet. The water in the bathtub is lukewarm but pleasurable and it erases, the soap erases the smells of airplanes and children crying, the long rows of expressionless faces lined-up to defecate, piss and wash. Another coat of soap and the train bubbles away, and the militaries salute, and the commuters slide down into the alarm call, and the dark-haired girl says for Massimo to wait tonight; tonight after her friends are asleep we will meet under the lamp post smack in the middle of the square in front of the station. No time to stay, places to go… tomorrow Massimo will go to visit Aunt Adriana, if she is there; he will ask her lover — everybody in the family knows that Uncle Joes is seeing her.

"Uncle Joes? Uncle Joes? I think I will see Aunt Adriana's place on Thursday." Twice "little one" repeats the phrase before his uncle hears him, only to beg him to stay longer before going off again.

"Don't worry, I will be back; now that I am studying in Rome, I will probably travel back and forth. I hope I get an apartment in Rome, I don't want to bother Aunt Adriana."

"It depends if they give you enough money for an apartment. They cost quite a bit. How much are they going to give you with that singing bursary anyway?"

"Slightly less than a thousand a month. Do you think I will be able to live off it, hey Uncle Joes?"

"When I was young we used to live off what the good God gave us... wait, the doorbell just rang..."

Udu is one year younger than Massimo, smaller in size. When they played together around the cathedral, about twenty years ago, Udu looked down upon the eager, question-filled friend and a smile would rise imperceptibly. Massimo laughed; they both made gurgled noises. Then Udu suggested they go and ring the nipples. Apart from that they ran inside the cathedral, shouting, kicking the soccer ball from one door to the other; or played hide-and-seek in the confessionals, underneath the altar, in one of the two crypts. Mainly they played soccer, beside the dome, and eyed from goal to goal, some of the blond-haired women that come and go, incessantly, day after day throughout the summer.

"It's Udu. He came to see you. I told him you would be arriving. Udu is here!" The sun is slowly setting behind the hills that one can embrace from the bathroom window. To accustomed eyes, the slowness conceals a fury that cannot be kept leashed, like horses grazing suddenly gallop and leap into a natural well. In fact, by the time Massimo emerges from the tub, laying rivulets around him, the evening star is already a focal point in the horizon. "Come on, lazy bones, get yourself dried. We'll go out to get something to eat, a bottle of wine, and we will listen to each other's seashell.''

"Always the poet, eh Udu?'' replies Massimo. "Have you published anything lately?''

Before their conversation arrives to the point when selective affinities start to ring in unison, Uncle Joes interrupts; a slight displeasure emerges from his hoarse voice:

"You have only been here two hours and already you are leaving. I was going to cook some supper for both of us...''

"Don't worry about it, Uncle Joes...'' An only nephew, he is wondering if he should stay or go with Udu. "There will be lots of times to eat together.''

"Please, if you are going to eat together, I will leave. I just thought that Massimo — wouldn't you Massimo — would have liked to embark upon a little journey up to the cathedral. We can go later, if you want!''

Massimo glances first towards his uncle, then seeing Udu, his slight and yet baffling smile, decides that he does not feel like listening to his uncle recount the day that his sister left with the *little one* to join her husband in Ontario, and the subsequent pain felt by his uncle. He winks to Udu and he tells him that he will be ready in a minute, while he disappears into the bedroom. By doing that, Massimo has tried to accomplish a variety of things that will not be understood. His uncle does not realize that he is three years older than the last time he came back, for in Uncle Joes' wrinkled mind time stops the moment his nephew departs.

Ed in un viaggio puo capitare di ritrovarsi a ricontare tutto quello che

> *hai perso quello che hai trovato quel*
> *che hai goduto quel che hai sprecato.*
>
> Claudio Lolli, *Viaggio*.

"The last time I saw you, it was down at the station and you said that the next time we would both be a little bald." Udu is impatient to have his friend readjust to time. Massimo, who is still sleepy, snaps out, only in intervals, from the daze of jet-lag. Around them, sprawled, sitting, composed and half-curious, the various mixture of the locals and the militaries, of newly-formed couples exchanging unmatched desires, of ex-boyfriends with turgid jeans, and the local bottle-drifters crouched heavily against the upper steps, uses the seven steps surrounding the cathedral's platform to gaze and be seen.

The two friends are still exchanging disconnected monologues when the local police car zooms a floodlight on their eyes. They pause annoyed and then resume, after a brief silence that like a pebble skims the surface of the last wave foaming on the sand, without losing their rhythm. It is a matter of minutes before, out-of-duty and bored, the uniformed officers interrupt the scene. The taller of the two uniforms (given the late hour and mixture of lights, the clothes stand out more than the man) asks briskly for documents. Massimo has left his Canadian passport in his room, he tells the John Wayne in front of him, and out of a self-induced stupor, partly fear and secondly politics, he babbles out that he is both an Italian and a Canadian, exempted from military duty; the certificate at home would prove this and that his address is correct, right? Udu produces out of his coat an identification card. Two cigarettes and a cigarillo flicker into the night, a small discussion ensues. But the boredom of the bearded gentlemen and the duty of the uniforms are released after a promise by Udu's companion to carry an identification card next time. With that, after two car doors slam in the now dark streets, the two comrades retrace their steps home by way of a very steep, very dark shortcut. "I find you changed," exclaims at one point Udu, "you seem to have lost your innocence. The last time you were here, three summers ago..."

"Three summers, three months... who cares? You too have changed." The shortcut has manoeuvred them into bidding a good-night, having fixed a rendezvous for the next day.

Udu, the formidable Udu who has taught Massimo the secrets of physical approaches; Udu, who at seventeen was living off Genova's homosexuals, who clicks at the sight of a shapely ass, once again shows the truth behind *travelling by sensation* (what Massimo acknowledges as intuition) when he leaped into the subject of displacement.

Apart from the few occasional pick ups of American, French and Chinese teenagers, wives of diplomats, lonesome sacks of hunger, they spend the next two weeks discussing identity, roots, displacement, whenever together. Their ideas and experience, in most instances, do not coincide, a poor formula for mutual understanding. Udu never overcame the boundaries, anthropological, invisible, of his hometown; Massimo is bound by the inner struggle of two languages. They make, for the first time, a tacit attempt to trade identities; but this leads only to more misunderstandings whenever Max's other half, the North American, surges up-front, in English, having stories to tell in that form.

It is at this point (one of stoic indignation, islands, fog and a circular current) that Udu befriends, after a quickie in a church's confessional, a German girl. A few leaves still cling to the linden trees; it is late November. Massimo has been spending, since October, most of his time at his aunt's place at the beach resort south of Rome. The conservatory in Rome, which he should be attending three times a week, has given place to an irregular life: late mornings, solitary singing, the occasional walk by the sea at two o'clock in the morning. There is always a half-filled bottle of white wine in the fridge, music papers are scattered about in the dining room, and a stench of cigarettes and wilted sexual dreams emanates from the bedroom walls. After all, the place where he is staying is rented out during the summer by his aunt who lives in Bologna most of the year. She considers the three-room apartment only as a source of secondary income; the pension as the widow of a war-hero lets her lead a comfortable life. Reminiscences, bridge with her girlfriends, all of them still alive, and on Saturday her manfriend pays a visit. Together they step lightly to the opera or to see the latest American movie, for they are both aficionados of classical art and unrepentant sustainers of the American way of life, which has so greatly contributed to Italy's emergence as the seventh major industrialized nation in the world, never mind the workers.

Aunt Adriana, Ms. Rapaci to her friends, has gone only once in the last ten years to visit Giove, as the village by the sea is called. On that occasion her fear of and disgust for the southerners surfaced for the last time when she called the train controller a Fascist-Communist for wanting to check her expired travel-reduction card. Her goodwill gesture to lend Massimo the mouse trap, as he calls it, was a God-given gift, for he will have to pay electricity and water, the garbage collectors' municipal taxes and the building maintenance expenses, since it is a condominium. The added bonus is that, probably, the break-ins (a once-every-two year affair) will drop dramatically by having there her nephew from America.

On one of his trips back to Trigliano, during the weekend (a journey of several hours, from sunset to one o'clock — a thousand sullen faces, the hypnotic clanking, and an occasional mystic, most often in a stupor, singer) Massimo, Max to his friends, is introduced to Udu's German live-in lover whom he will address as Lucia, the light bearer. Thus, what was once a duo becomes a trio; for in Lucia Max will finally realize that he has more than one soul, as the ancients called the ghosts in man, and that these phantasms speak very different languages. "Every time you come back, you spend your time with Udu's fiancee, especially now that he is working, everybody will..." Early Friday morning, Massimo cuts Uncle Joes' speech in half with an alright, alright, we are all friends who share something special; and that, no, there is nothing going on behind Udu Marianelli's back and that, yes, he is spending time with them because they are the only people that he can relate to. Of course, the fact that Mr. Pavonazzi has rented the downstairs apartment to his nephew's comrades does not help; yet, it was a good-will gesture for Udu, who turned thirty November first, and who gave up seasonal work and living with his parents to find a job in the municipal bureaucracy as an accountant so as to be an equal in Regina's nest.

II
Andante

*And the sun pours down like honey
on our Lady of the Harbour, and she
shows you where to look, among the
garbage and the flowers.*

L. Cohen,
"Suzanne."

*Mare mare mare voglio annegare
portami lontano a naufragare via via
via da queste sponde portami lontano sulle onde.*

Franco Battiato,
"Summer on a Solitary Beach."

"Hi. The key was in the lock, so I just walked in."

"Hello Maxy. Would you like an espresso... no, you
don't drink espresso, that is right. Would you like a cup of
warm chocolate, perhaps?"

"That's o.k. Reg... Lucia. I want to call you in Italian... I, I'll just watch you drink your coffee. You know I
like tosèe you thiswày, clàdin spring garn mènts: a
greenànd bluestripèd ped towel. The hair-àir wet bythe
shower ofan earlyrain..."

"Oh, stop it," chuckles Regina as Massimo imitates
accents, "You shouldn't make fun of Udu's light verse
that way. He likes you very much. He is always thinking of
writing a song with you."

"I didn't mean to make fun of him, I can only sing... baritone at that, and I..."

"Why don't you sit down instead of standing there?"

Accomplices in the great danger of a platonic friendship, Massimo and Regina spend mornings skipping from English to Italian, having fun with French. It is stimulating for Udu's pal to have someone to confide in; after two months of voluntary absentia from dwelling in ideas, subjects, crossword puzzles, he has someone who laughs at his jokes, his English puns, and who listens and nods, offering counter points to his constructions; someone who shares his hatred for the Americans and their way of life.

Bona fide intellectuals, who delve in politics (Lucia was a member of the Green Party in Germany, and she actually knew a woman who gave refuge to Bader and Meinhoff in Rome, at the beginning of their careers) can be horrified by absolute principles and yet, fascinated by the self-imposed certainty, the categorical division "us and them," that permeates any group convinced that Europe has been invaded by the malignant cancer called U.S.A. and to which all the evils of the world, from Khomeni to Coke, can be traced.

Strolling at noon, from the cathedral to Udu's office, (hidden in one of the Etruscan streets, in the heart of the ancient part of Trivigliano's hill) along the Corso Cavour, Maxy is bent on a self-purging soliloquy: "You know, if I had stayed here, in Italy, I am sure I would have joined the *Naps*. I know, the Red Brigades made a universal mistake. His release would have crippled the system... think of it, the Christians having to abandon the coalition. Finally we could have defeated the Mafia, instead of tapping their lines... and, and the C.I.A. would have gone back to growing peanuts. They should kill all of them, the bastards!"

"What about the fact that they brought about this not-so-subtle repression? Isn't that self-defeating for the Movements? And death, death, death to uniforms and to poor peasants' boy. Death, the great cleaning agent..."

It is at this point that Maxy loses track of Lucia's innuendos, her thirst for a fall, an endless fall back into the placenta, conscious, forgiving. To him, she is being metaphysical, like Americans are cold and superficial, like Italians, yes, Italians are chaotic, sensuals, liars, mystical. Spaces of silence float between their words, sudden bursts of identities wanting to confirm themselves, to reach beyond their little azurine fog, the polished and ragged contours of rocks drifting, drifting and colliding, surging to stop, stopping to lose themselves in puddles of lava and rain, wreckage of hours, of flesh adding to itself new flesh, of rocks drifting in the fog.

"There is mon amour, Udu." The sudden burst of excitement in Regina's voice, still trembling off the trampoline of irony, catches Massimo off guard, imbued in his resentment for the Americans. Udu walks slowly towards them, with his nonchalant gait favouring the left leg, dull remembrance of a polio attack when he was fourteen. Lucia is quick to notice by a spring of half-seconds her lover's mood on hearing them conversing in English; she reverts to Italian, offsetting Massimo's rhythm in a joyful embrace.

"Why don't we go to Bolsena to eat some fish. We can take the car and be there in twenty minutes." Massimo is not sure of Udu's offer; Uncle Joes will have probably set the table by now; it is two o'clock... But the two transcultural lovers, after the simple suggestion to phone and let his uncle know, manage to convince Maxy. It is a beautiful day, warm, the sky is a brilliant blue; it rained the last four days, and he and his uncle can come down to spend New Year's day with them, and not to forget to get some of Uncle Joes' wine from the cellar; two bottles will be fine for a delicious dinner.

Christmas holidays: for Massimo now in the fourth month of his vacation, this is the time when he should feel homesick. In a peculiar, yet enchanting way, his parents have been replaced by Udu and Lucia — Udu, who when Lucia is off in one of her morbid, solitary, moods to walk about a stranger in her shadow, somewhere in the meanders of Trigliano's woods and streets, is still capable of a quickie with a tourist enticed by an American "hello"; Lucia, who breaks the trio with escapes into forests, as she calls them, black forests of *Nostalgia*, like a heroine in a silent Russian movie.

February rolls short of completing its duty. The snow, the coldest winter in two centuries, is still in a lover's embrace with roofs, streets, branches. The Carnival has just goofed its donkey-hoofs in the last Thursday of jokes, confetti, plastic green or red white-striped batons. Massimo, coming from the station, jumps from step to step the staircase that leads to his chums' apartment.

"Hello... *Vieles erlebt ich, obgleich die Locke Jugendlich wallet mir um die Schlafe!*" Massimo shouts to the tune of "When the Saints Come Marching In", making his way through the door. "A girl on the train just taught me that. What does it mean, hey Lucia?" He doesn't quite notice that his friends are in a sour mood, slowly eating their vegetable soup, as if to sustain an inner warmth through the spoon and the steaming bowl.

"It means that you have cut many vicissitudes out of your class and that your curls swing from a beer-tree, you wild youth." Lucia lights up with this answer, in the secret hope that Udu, "Kleiner" as she calls him, will throw one of his jokes in the air, and with it his bad feelings.

"Why don't you eat with us?" Kleiner's suggestion is left hanging while Maxy, excited, tells them that he has just received a letter from Mary.

"Who is Mary?" asks Udu. Lucia has stopped eating the green soup.

"She is the one, the one I have been in love with for the last nine years."

"The one who married a few years ago, with someone younger than her; the blonde married to a street cleaner...?" Udu is quicker than Regina to recollect from Massimo's stories, the right character, the virginal blonde who danced through Max's cluster of veins.

"Yes, just the one," Massimo blurts out, joining the previous half of a burp to the other.

"She just wrote me in Giove. She is coming the seventeenth of March." Max goes on to answer that she will be staying with him for a couple of weeks before her brother will come to carry her off to Morocco, sometime in April.

What is love? One could ask together with Regina, who does not deny the flesh an adventure, limited in time and space. A variety of answers could ensue, depending on one's list of books on the matter; the lovers of Buscaglia would certainly agree with his typology that it is an embrace. Udu, cynical, pragmatic, sensual, would have jealousy as a substitute, for malice has whispered in his ears that his companions have indulged, while he is at work, in some passion, because of his leg. Love, in Massimo's cage of ribs, is the act of making love to love. Between the ideal and the anus, between the drinking bouts with Udu alone and the liver's call for food, there is Mary. Mary, who never knew he loved her nine years ago. Mary, who will settle after her divorce (she told Massimo the second day in Giove), with the father of her child-to-be. Love, like Harlequin Romance shows, is risk, like Pavarotti breaking his throat for fame and fortune, never mind Caruso. Love is Mary, who has waited five years for her husband to make her into a woman, to produce what Udu asserts to be a woman's priority. Sperm, the arrows and the hot air balloon, the egg, the snake and the apple enticed to dance a tango, a millenium of boogie-woogies, replicas. Love is Massimo who rediscovers, after prostitutes, some unpaid for, the conjunction of the ghost and the blood in Mary.

"Touch me, there, there!" Maximo commands; Mary wills herself to obey. Obey, after the freedom of a too understanding husband; obey after the impotence of a blank diary, the scratched title of which is "Mytia, my son;" obey and enjoy his tongue darting around your lips, not quite sure of the pleasure-bud's position, the lips two wings to trace the way home to the nest, while the sweat of an impossible birth is still circling your pupils. Mary, Mary, why did you slip into his bed the first night you arrived? A platonic friendship is possible only between latent homosexuals in this country.

Mary is off to Rabat. Maximo, whom she left in Rome's station, is singing to himself, softly like a mother, in the empty compartment back to Trigliano. Today is a late Easter Sunday that only a few Christians celebrate, shut off in their dull, repetitive lives. She has left most of her bags behind, in Giove. He, one day of the three weeks of lucid delirium, of waiting, of practicing the vocal scales for an impending exam, after Udu picks up two French girls (Lucia is back in Berlin for a visit), refuses the flesh for the ideal he has been practicing for. "*Je m'excuse, mais c'est que... je suis amoureux et je ne veux pas tromper mon amour.*" Marianne clads herself with a skirt, trips in the darkness over the music stool beside the bed, where clothes are thrown, and rejoins her friend Joanne, who is by now sixty-nining Udu downstairs. It is the right decision, thinks Massimo, imbued with fatalism and self-deception.

"I have something to tell you." Mary has just stepped off the train from Naples, and after the kiss that Maximo has been waiting for, she makes his nightmares breathe in his lungs. They are in the Station's bar; in Maximo's hand there is a glass of vodka. In front of Mary, a cup of espresso is releasing an imperceptible windmill of steam. She will take her bags and go back to Morocco. She has met a car dealer from France with whom she has fallen in love.

"Let us talk about it. I love you!" The imposition shreds the silence between the islands of their faces like a blade on a neck, the revolution over but for the fingerprints of a child to come and disappear through their lips.

"I am staying, I am... staying because I don't want to hurt him. Soon, though, I will go back to Maurice." May, the month of the Virgin; the celebration of the workers' day with Regina back in Italy; this time she can confide in her newfound friend, Mary. Massimo and Udu are exchanging mnemonic parenthesis from their flirt with life, near the cathedral, in a bar, eying this year's crop of local produce. Regina and Mary are in Regina's kitchen, two individuals, surrounded by walls, lovers, ghosts. Lucia has just finished retelling Mary of her Greek lover in Berlin, Mary of hers in Morocco. They both agree to stay a while yet, so as not to hurt their lovers' feelings.

"I want to leave. I chose him. I don't have his address in Morocco. I want to see him; he was good to me."

"Why?" Massimo asks. "Why? I love you!" Paolo's Bar has welcomed them once again, the eighth time this week; on their table glasses of beer, "Grand Marnier," champagne bind their fury with opacity. Mary will keep taking her decisions to stay, week after week, until the fourth of July, before going back to Canada and sacrificing her wants for the ultimate in an intimate friendship — a friendship that Maximo mistakes for love, duty confused with passion, sex with God.

The quartet between May and July, when Regina will also leave for good to join her boyfriend in Berlin, has an extraordinary capacity to absorb details, minute but important details, dispelled by Udu's mimicry and jokes.

"We heard you this afternoon. The bed cranked like a train jolted out of its tracks..." Mary is in the kitchen, and listens, still blushing from her lovemaking bout, to Udu, who makes fun, poetically, of Maximo's appetite. She shies away but is half-enticed by this Italian hearsay voyeurism. After a few minutes, having taken a shower, Max is laughing with the three of them.

III
Adagio

*Bevi la coca cola che ti fa bene bevi
la coca cola che ti fa digerire con
tutte quelle, tutte quelle bollicine...
bbrrilllll*

> Vasco Rossi,
> "Bollicine."

*I want you. I want you, I want you so
bad. Honey, I want you.*

> Bob Dylan,
> "I want you."

*Reloj, no marques las horas porque
voy a enloquecer... Ella es la estrella
que alumbre mi ser, yo sin su amor
no soy nada.*

> Manuel Scorza
> «Reloj de Medianoche,
> in *La Danza Inmovil*.

"I am pregnant!" The excitement in Mary's voice, through a cable thousands of miles away, jolts Maximo's nerves.

"You are?... I knew it. I dreamed about it after you left. It was that day on the beach, wasn't it?"

"I can't talk any longer; this is not my phone."

"Where are you staying?"

"With my folks!"

"I passed my exams... I love you!"

The telephone clicks. The telephone clicks and the line parrots the hum of the silence between Massimo's rib cage and his penis. Massimo's muscle is slicing petals with desire, the petals of the rose bush entwined with the railings and the steps underneath, that lead to Uncle Joes' apartment. He goes out on the balcony, leaving the living room's light on, and breathes in deep the summer of stars, of poisonous fire flies, five about, and rushes downstairs to announce the news to his friends. They open a bottle of Uncle Joes' wine. It is the third week in July; Lucia is about to go back, definitely, to Berlin. Massimo's concern for himself didn't let Regina's statement about her nullified situation infiltrate his love.

Three days later Massimo and Udu are once again the fox and the wolf of the dome's steps. A few hours of unfruitful search for sex, makes them decide that it is time to go to Giove, to the beach, to the women alone, with husbands still working in Rome. Trigliano, in the sunset fog, is a hill of tufa encircled by the railway, an island, mute, still; only the cathedral is visible. Once in Giove, they clean Massimo's apartment; the second night, at midnight, they rush nude into the ocean's waters as Lucia and Mary called the Tyrrhenian Sea. Max and Kleiner laugh their way back into the apartment, to the bathroom and the shower. They have carried a half-filled bottle of Trigliano white with them to take a shower, to wash the sand off their bodies. Sips of wine are mixed with soap and water, laughter; one is a father-to-be, the other a bachelor again, with the possibilities of an empty apartment.

From Canada, Massimo sends this letter to Regina, bringing her up-to-date with nine months of silent footfalls, of a cracked throat, of banks of white angst.

"This is Canada: roots, chewed, munched, vomited and sour. And the shout in everybody's breast, surging forward against death's sickle. Like Udu made the immigrants up to be: poor jerks, with an accent, southerners, peasants, shepherds... I have been seeing them, singing to them, in cultural centres, in the church and at weddings with a rock band. Me, the Piped Piper of idiots, in love with their folly, with their tears and their villages back home. Making fun of them, imitating their accent, spying their third generation football players and virgins with equal somatic features, with gold chains and amulets, not knowing Italian but for some strange dialect. Sons of sons of escaped Fascists, who still carry Mussolini's photograph in their wallet like the school director I worked for. Idiots, who will marry bakers, secretaries, cooks who only know that Italy won over West Germany in the soccer's World Cup final, in 1982. Udu told me that I have lived here too long. Thirteen years, one more than the stations of the Cross... Do you remember the revolution? Bruno Conti's cross to Altobelli for the first Italian goal? and how the German defence opened its legs to let the shot through, filling up the net with a giant roar... and Pertini waving, bricklayers, pseudo-mafiosi connected to New York via relations of blood and pasta, storekeepers with an ulcer, madmen with roses blooming in their mouths, writing poetry on blank faces, fat women who are not fat, with a mustache line along their anus cracks, afraid to die after a masectomy, having cried silently for weeks, without a word to anyone, only to find out that it was a benign beauty spot... I watch these men, and women, gyrating their orbits out of the cafe's windows, out of kitchens with cellophane insulation over the windowpanes, with majestic decorations of fake marble and fake tiles, out of their children's mouths, wide open to see the blond-haired Virgin give birth to a Botticelli's shell & venus believing the name to be a wine from the North, from Valtellina, from Turin, from someone who speaks a different dialect, half-educated, producing radio programs that surround a boot, made of leather... back to the fifties with Elvis Presley! Back to the March to Rome! Back to the caves, with fists dirtied with blood and glistening tufts of hair. Marinetti, shocked elbows, black Camaros! I have lived here too long? It is only now that I understand them, tell that to our comrade Udu... I came back, not able to speak their language. The idiots, the idiots. Me, with this voice like a sax... self-righteous kind. Anglos, angles in my throat, stuffing the frog in my throat... self-righteous. You should have seen her, a whale in her belly, cooking for her folks, remember? she never cooked in Giove or Trigliano. A woman with a nest in her legs, with L.S.D. in her womb, spiders picking one by one each red pubic hair, braiding five years and an egg into completion. My sperm... my sperm... me in Ottawa going from the cafes to a chess set! Checkmated, I was out of the game. I walked looking for a menial job, a father-to-be without a place, save for his parents' book up-turned, a pyramid, a bed. Twist and shout, back to the sixties... back to the sixties with poppies! My baby, she was having my baby, like Paul Anka's Polish-Italian-Anglo-Canadian-Armenian-Bobby-Vinton-Adam-Smiths was having his. No jobba, no worka, no nothing... Do you like my imitation? like Udu's mimicry? It was not long ago that we four sat down in your kitchen to shoot the shit... I was Mary's scapegoat; it is a movie starring all of us, right? I was a scapegoat; Lucia! the scapegoat of my love of symbols. Three, nine, five and seven, four numbers to spin the head into a Virgo's horoscope, who turned twenty-five at the end of July. Perfect numbers invisible... Music is the perfect system, pain and joy in symbols: *tra-la-la-lala*! We broke off soon after I came back: Possession! I changed the rules like you changed your rules with Udu, Kleiner right? Only, you left because you wanted to, like always, like only you can... remember? what did you ever find in your solitary walks, oh Rousseau, to make a long story short I am not the father of this *baby*... I prepared myself for nine months. Waiting, hoping already full with Italian, my background Christ, to give to it. It, the baby, the ca, the es, in my throat... like a frog. I have a frog in my mouth, a baby frog in my throat. Anyway I am matching you, going over you: I am none, no one now! I let go of my studies after I couldn't find a job: Imagine; me, a worker! part of the proletariat! I told her I was going to Kitchener or Waterloo, an emblem of kitsch like all Italo-Canadians, to work in a factory...! This was before she broke off completely. I found out: I phoned for days, weeks, knowing that her time was due, every hospital in the City! She used me to make up with her ex-husband, the dog-faced patroller, the bastard I'm sure. Anyway, I found out like John Lennon, my mother went to see her mother... mothers defending scarred vaginas. She wouldn't talk to me at all, no phone no letters no chickory Mr. Lombardi! the baby, she had another lover when she came back; she didn't shy from sending a letter in November saying that our baby was due in March... A little girl, with my ears it seemed, a little girl, Christ, with a black leather skirt, like her mother... I am off, somewhere. Hope to see you in my dreams, but I keep hearing the train... derailing. I wake up in the middle of every night. Sweat! and this December... it is the coldest in centuries, minus forty every night... not able to sleep again. Anyway, see you... Maximo...''

Remembrances. Regina, Lucia, after two years with Udu and Max, with a young boy who, like Max, has black curly hair and green eyes, named Alexander in memory of her husband's father is still writing to Udu, Lieben Kleiner. They have kept, beside the incidents in their paths criss-crossed, a keen resemblance for life elsewhere. Today Regina is all alone in the house; her husband has taken Alexander to the Berlin Zoo. It is Saturday afternoon; she is crying softly to herself, going back two years. Udu's letter arrived this afternoon; he says that he met Uncle Joes; he told Udu that Massimo had died a week before. Lucia walks slowly to the bathroom; her stomach is swelling up with last night's hamburgers, one way to make little Alexander happy. As she steps into the bathroom, her eyes watery, feverish, like a cobweb, Lucia picks up from the sink a few curly black hairs. When Alexander and his father will walk into the tiny apartment, there will be Udu's letter on the brown carpet, and a letter, written in English, a language they do not understand, marking the fiftieth page of William Blake's *Poems and Prophecies*; a naked woman, plumpish, her wrists cut, is seated beside the toilet, her arms perfectly balanced in a crimson sunset water.

Regina's unmailed letter, dated the 29th of January, 1986, was addressed to Massimo. I read:

Ciao. *I am writing from Berlin as you can see. Sorry I do not write before. Hope everything is working according to its plan. The stories take place with a syntax we cannot appreciate. The flux, that is what we contained. Every-thing else is surfaces, wine, mirrors. Morals, aesthetics, want to embank it. Psychologism, an imitation; you can-not blow breath into clay. So you have been father. Is there a joy? Was it willed, a common agreement? Do not tell me that each is prey of a call to duplicate a deviance, Maxy, always a deviance. Are we so enthralled with the mirror in our heaven, in our hell, that we step into twilight to fanta-size our looks? As confusing as I can be: down with vi-tality, up with the moon's behind! Relax, sweet. Hold your picture away from the hearts, sacrifice it; let dead gods wallow in your veins. The blood is all, the blood, not the temples. Dream is now buried deep underneath the pavement? Were you there, sperm and slogans? You played with numbers: three, nine, subdivisions, multipli-cations. Of course she was beautiful, more than Fay Dunaway. It made you stand out, Prince Charming. Yet, you lose, the world did not conform to your full desire. As such you need not involve yourself with neurotics.*

Consider for an eternal moment the Gioconda. Was she happy because of triangles she was part of? Probably she did not even know that a pyramid is a flat triangle. I do not even know where these are going. I was jovially upset at your lack of news, comrade. We will meet again. Here, let us place remembrances (I am tired to apostrophize all the negatives!) *which are with us, in the book of life. Have a laugh, and sing me a Lieben. That is what is most en-dearing about you, Max, that you will make fun of every-thing even after we are dust and yellow photographs in an album, somewhere in Borges' collection; right? Leave the Canadians, our Americans, to their trees. Coleridge bles-sed the water snakes; can you not make provisions for those manmocks? She was beautiful in her innocence. So what?*

You, no money, no honey. Is it not, Innocence, inhuman in the world? Suppose an Angel, the Angel from Kingdom-come-to-zero-hour did in fact exist. Good golly Miss Molly; just one, this one, would be alien enough to wipe the human kind clean. Off with trees, off with grass, off with the Giant Phallic Mush. Then there would be plenty of Room for Recrimination. She let the Angel out of her womb. Imagine it, if you can; the lips part, two drenched wings, immediately dry in the Spring's air carry off a fiery Sword into the Abyss! I wonder if you have considered (excuse our passion for capitals) birth giving like this, and, anyway Maxy, what of experience? Recriminations and Nostalgia a cocktail more powerful than a Bloody Mary or a Zombie. Bear with me, I felt like addressing the Union. No more tunnels, no more trains to take, only feet and hands in the sunshine, like a baby without a name, exploding form the darkness, right Maxy?

With Love, Lucia.

SANTE A. VISELLI

Ed io anche son pittore

Strange that Dante should have forgotten the immigrant circle! Many years have already passed since you left the wretched village you loved so much, the houses behind the church standing like old mourners at a funeral. Remember. The month of May we used to recite the rosary. Evenings fire-flies broke the silence of our looks. A song disappeared on a bicycle under the auspices of a poverty that was sacrilegious. As for you, indifferent Ocean. Charon seized the immigrant with a relentless fever and, as in Greek mythology, the old captain set us ashore on this rock where every day nostalgia eats at our hearts. Nostalgia for what? Of a picture a little too romantic to be true; of feelings left behind forever; of a hedge too white to be covered with snow...

An immigrant strolls along this irregular coast. The Ocean, humanity's enemy, separates him from reality. The hard-to-forget cry of a fisherman who was swallowed last year at Portugal Cove has touched only your feelings. The same day people at the marketplace were complaining: "This fish is too dear!" "Is the lobster fresh?" In Terranova even scandal is a form of snobbery. In the Mediterranean the poor man might have saved himself.

These vain thoughts take me back to when the new world appeared before us like a paradise-inferno. I began at that time a diary: "In here I will write everything I hear, all my thoughts, joys and sorrows, not because I think myself important, but because I want to be able to relive some day this ephemeral, senseless youth." I never again took up the pen, not wanting to reveal to the world my frustration; the events of my life I imprinted with my loneliness on my immigrant's heart: down in a mine, in refineries, in kitchens, at university or along the shore of Terranova. Today I look on this expanse and talk to Guglielmo Marconi. On Signal Hill overlooking the port of St. John's they have dedicated a commemorative plaque. Even he is shocked to hear the sweet idiom of his native land. Together we send messages across from this reef: the wind answers in English. The event heartens us; besides what's the sense of changing history? The sun sets, and we are ready to die; Caboto and Verrazano went this same way. It's strange! Canada is a bilingual country.

Last night I wanted to hear a friends' voice:

"Pietro, how are you?"

"Fine; I can't complain. When are you coming to Toronto?"

Strange! Fifteen years ago he asked the same thing. Toronto, a sort of corrupt surrogate. Friends for life, we can get together only by telephone. Too busy to listen to our hearts. Too stupid to recognize ourselves as impratical dreamers, we say there will be other occasions. Another fisherman died today in the bay. The price of fish goes up, people complain. The mine...

Yes, I had forgotten. Of course, after this sea voyage I tend to be forgetful. I am stiff, inhumanly so — into rigor mortis; perhaps there is life at the bottom of the Ocean.

I begin to get nervous; my conversation is fragmented, though today is almost a nice day and my mind, warmed by an occasional lost ray, is fertile with ideas. An immigrant remembers everyting so — in bits and pieces; even his speech is a linguistic monster, indiscriminate, with no emotion. Except the mine...

Be patient, Alessandro! I am still in Winnipeg and the trip is long and hopeless. I look and look again at a photo, at the ghostly face of someone far away, a fleeting reminder of hate and love, attractions, and remembrances of an old crumbling house inseparable from that of a mother embraced for the last time at the Polyclinic. Tears? Reasonable people don't cry. I am a Pygmalion in reverse. Silence. Even my blood is quiet and sluggish, perhaps subdued by this immense forest swarming with flies. Big trees and small, thin ones that look like spaghetti for an old Indian *chaudière*. I remember a song; I used to sing it when I was hungry: *Roma mia, tutta mia, tu sei un piatto di pasta e poesia, sul vassoio più grande del mondo c'è un cucchiaio per tutti...* I don't remember the rest. On the road to Thompson, I.N.C.O., Falcon Bridge they wait for us... pasta no longer rhymes... poetry comes in white. Tomorrow a kilometer underground we'll search for an answer to our agony. The sun has betrayed us. Light has no

111

language, only an impenetrable transparency. Behind its wall of pretense and ambitions I've hidden my madness, the misunderstood grief in my eyes, the perennial face of death, the sacred message of the guilty, the fierce judgement of the newborn. On the No. 6, in Manitoba, it's hot. The wind from the east is choking. My Charger seems to bend under the weight of my foot: 120 miles an hour to be on time at the mine. Immigrants can't be late; their excuses are not accepted. I'll try to sing a little now. Alessandro, do you remember this song? You've stayed a dreamer, human... whereas I...

Quando il vento dell'est mi porterà
il profumo dei capelli suoi
Io guarderò verso il vento dell'est
e mi ricorderò che lei è andata di là
Quando il vento dell'est si fermerà
e la neve verrà a posarsi su noi
Se sarà lì con te fa che non pianga mai
che non abbia mai freddo che non soffra mai più
E perché i suoi capelli sian sempre più lunghi
Perché solo così e più bella che mai

Io guarderò verso il vento dell'est
E mi ricorderò
Per vederla tornar.

It's a touching lyric; I'm almost moved. Pietro — my classmate at Frosinone's technical high school and my workmate in the mine — can barely hide his tears. I tell him: you're a miner by profession, an honest lawyer — which is to say without clients — at present an electrician. Me... a miner *jeegaboo* — or as my French professor at the University of Manitoba would say — *un petit Italien de*

rien du tout, an electrician who never had a job and a bad
poet. When something I say or do seems good to the
English, they shower me with flattering compliments:
"That's not too bad for a wop." Pietro and Santino... the
two best friends in the world. Our friendship is paradoxi-
cal. We see one another every five or six years, talk about
metaphysics and our electronics professor — because he
always used to say *putacaso*, suppose, he was nicknamed
Professor Putacaso — then we talk about politics, of the
whores of Verano, of whether it might not be useful to re-
open the brothels. We agree about nothing. Our friendship needs no explanations.

May nights were intense in my village. *Chitarra suona
più piano, qualcuno può sentire, soltanto lei deve capire...
soltanto lei che a quest'ora stringe il cuscino e sospira.* Like
when I used to go with Alessandro and Didier to the beach
at Carnon, near Montpellier, to chase after girls in topless
bikinis. Yes, Alessandro. There must have been times
when you too had a tune in your head. I couldn't get her
out of my mind. Her parents didn't approve; I came from
a poor family. Her letter never came. The postal strike...
She still has my heart, even on this side of the Ocean, on
the prairies. *Aca nada.* How many times during afternoon
walks to Castelli Romani, over a light lunch — a bread roll
stuffed with *porchetta* and a glass of *frizzantino d'Aprilia*
— did we dream of the American prairies? Here everything we do violates Nature. Before joining you at the University of Manitoba, I couldn't imagine the dimensions of
this huge billiard table. Every day at the corner of Via
Tiburtina we used to buy comic books about cowboys and
Indians, gold prospectors and fur traders — a naive picture
erased by reality; instead, we stand before a class of philosophy students, teach them the concept of liberty. I

know, it's an old cliche: that we no longer know how to dream. Today, to quote the poet Carducci, we know "how to read *about* Greek and *about* Latin," and we write, write, write... I think of the cypress trees around the village cemetery, where my grandmother rests. I was working in a mine in Manibridge when I received news of her death. With her last breath she wished me at her bedside. I am her husband's namesake. I can speak of her today only with tenderness; in deep gloom and the pretense that one puts up in a foreign land, I remember the simple goodness of her face, her prayers, her blessing on my departure from the port of Naples, the enchanted surprise in her gestures on seeing me again unexpectedly three years later, in the month of May. How beautiful is this month in my village! My father sent me this song. I sing it, playing my guitar, though I changed the ending:

> *Paese mio che stai sulla collina*
> *disteso come un vecchio addormentato*
> *la noia e l'abbandono sono la tua malattia*
> *Paese mio ti lascio Io vado via*
>
> *Che sarà, che sarà, che sarà*
> *Che sarà della mia vita chi lo sa*
> *So far tutto o forse niente*
> *Da domani si vedrà*
> *Che sarà, che sarà, quel che sarà*
>
> *Gli amici miei son quasi tutti via*
> *Ed altri partiranno dietro me*
> *Peccato perché stavo bene in loro compagnia*
> *Ma tutto passa, tutto se ne va*
>
> *Che sarà, che sarà, che sarà*
> *Che sarà della mia vita chi lo sa*

114

Con me porto la chitarra
E se la notte piangerò
Una nenia di paese suonerò

Amore mio ti bacio sulla bocca
Che fu la fonte del mio primo amore
Ti do l'appuntamento dove e quando non lo so
Ma so soltanto che
Non *ritornerò*.

Noticed the change? An immigrant can't go back. During his wanderings only the guitar, his one friend, can understand his feelings at will: manners, meanings and strange behaviour. We are made up mainly of emotion. And bitter are the pleasures of the unknown. Aeneas' companions were not greeted with: *"Italiam! Italiam!"* Neither will we be... Ours... *Aca nada*... Laugh, *pagliaccio*. A wolf dashes across our path.

A voyage into the unknown can become a lesson in philosophy. It was at night that I was first fascinated by the Canadian forest. As I was driving back to the mining camp from Snow Lake, a wolf appeared on the road in front of the car. A noble face, with a challenging look, without trace of fear. His whole bearing suggested a life of struggle to survive, of hunger, attacks, victories, defeats, death, freedom. Free, without reason, logic or philosophy, I saw him move away finally. Alone, swallowed by his mysterious forest, he disappeared into the darkness of his world, leaving me with a strange insight, saddened: that all progress whether through space and time or in thought is but the illusion of being still enamoured of fixed stars. Man's cry against the universe — an ignoble shriek with occult notes from a throat strangled by fear of the unknown — is pathetic, insignificant. An immigrant does not know how

115

to listen to *le cri du loup*. Like a rich leper, hidden in his own house, unknown even to his own family, invisible, he is betrayed by is own voice. On the road to the mine, that day, I learned to face death.

That same morning I went down the shaft and, as usual, began to work furiously. But in the darkness I saw a wolf's eyes. I remember. The poem "Gli Aquiloni" by Pascoli:

C'è qualcosa di nuovo oggi nel sole
Anzi d'antico
Io vivo altrove
Ma sento che sono
Intorno nate le viole.

It's a poem about death. A poem about a Metaphysical Miner is... I don't know... perhaps a poem about remembrances, dreams, challenges — of threatening Nature's stone heart, in the hope of softening it, with dynamite, with violence, with a beam of light. Or, simply, it's a poem about an immigrant, about Pietro or maybe about Alessandro. Maybe my colourless painting.

My eyes search for the last ship swallowed by the fog. The Grand Banks of Terranova are far, my family warm, though the sun has forgotten us: "*Italiam, Italiam!*" No one answers. Even Guglielmo Marconi is dozing. "Where's my son? I don't see him." Dante forgot the circle for misled immigrants. Inferno, on a reef in the Ocean. Charon walks on water — another miracle in reverse — to protect me from the living and the past. Sitting on this jutt of land — not certainly Gargano's — I wait for the sun. The crossing has been a revelation. Will this voyage be the last? Always the same vain question. May, month of flowers and

116

death; yours is the geographical modulation. Even the sky cried that day, cloudless though it was; not just a mother who saw her fisherman son drawn up from the Ocean's bowels; not she who said good-bye from a hospital bed. My Italian heart revolts. Even Marconi has turned his shoulders to Europe. Tomorrow I will return to this reef. We will continue to send messages, though Italy does not reply to exiles. Until tomorrow, old globe... Always to an old friend.

Translated from the Italian by C.D. Minni.

JOHN BENSON

For Maria with Love

Soon after the end of the Second World War Toni emigrated from a small village in Calabria — a remote, poverty-stricken place on the sun-baked toe of Italy.

Toni was constantly wiping his face to clear the rivulets of sweat that bubbled and oozed from the folds of his skin.

Although he looked aggressive, the wrinkles that spread out from the corners of his eyes belied the pugnacious line of his blue-tinted jaw and battered, boxer's nose. He spoke shattered English in a hoarse grumble that started down where his enormous belly bulged over his belt.

I first met Toni when I had been out on an assign-
ment in the back streets of the East Side. At the time I
worked for a newspaper that liked to portray the seamy
side of life, and they don't come any seamier than the East
Side of our city. It was a cold, wet night and I seemed to be
quite alone on the deserted streets. I was tired and hungry
and, I don't mind admitting, more than a little apprehen-
sive. If I was carrying a wad of money it wouldn't have
mattered so much, but it seemed a pity to get my throat
cut for the few dollars I had in my wallet.

The light filtering through the grimy, steam-covered
window of Toni's cafe was a welcome sight. As I pushed
through the door a bell attached to the lintel clanged
noisily. The noise didn't disturb the only other customer
who sprawled, asleep or stupefied, across one of the stained
marble tables.

The cafe was like a hundred, a thousand such places:
half a dozen tables and an assortment of battered chairs; to
one side a counter dominated by a battered, steaming urn
and a glass case containing a few hazardous pies and an
assortment of brightly coloured cakes.

As I sat down on one of the stools that fronted the
counter Toni appeared from the back regions. He pulled
out a rag that was tucked into the apron strings around his
waist and proceeded to wipe the counter top. Without
raising his head to look at me he said, ''What you want?''

Feeling equally disinclined for small talk I said tersely,
''Coffee!''

Toni paused in his labours, placed the rag very de-
liberately on the counter, hunched his shoulders, spread
his huge arms wide and turned up his palms in a gesture of
despair. Punctuating each word with a little nod of his
head, he said to the world at large, ''Coffee he says! What

sorta coffee? Black coffee — with cream — with sugar — without sugar — cappuccino — espresso?''

I was tired and irritable. "Cappuccino," I snapped.

He shook his balding head from side to side. His double chins swayed in contra-motion. "You get what I got and what I got is black — with or without sugar!''

I laughed despite myself. Toni paused and looked at me for a moment, sizing me up. His eyes disappeared behind the folds of their lids. His head went back. His stomach and his chins started to vibrate. Toni roared until the tears ran down his cheeks and the prostrate customer stirred uneasily.

Toni reached over the counter and patted my shoulder. "You are O.K. — you I like!'' He pushed a cup of coffee in front of me and then, bending below the counter, brought out a bottle. "For you is black coffee,'' he chuckled. "And good Italian brandy. No charge — on the house!''

A strange phenomenon sometimes occurs. Two men — strangers — alike or unalike in colour, race or creed, immediately establish a relationship like brothers — perhaps even stronger than that. So it was with Toni and me. On that first meeting we talked about football and footballers, politicians and pimps, women and wars — until we had finished the brandy and the first streaks of daylight filtered through the window.

Whenever I was in the district I would call in for a coffee and a gossip. Often, as at our first meeting, we would sit all night talking or sometimes playing two-handed brag or checkers.

On occasions I had noticed a woman working in the kitchen behind the cafe. She was a big-breasted, peroxide blonde in her late twenties or early thirties . She would

121

have been quite a looker if she hadn't used a shovel to apply her make-up. Sometimes she was there; sometimes she wasn't.

One night I said something to Toni about his wife not working that night — or something like that. Toni looked puzzled. His hands worked overtime. His hands always worked overtime — without his hands he would have been dumb.

He said, "I've got no wife here."

I started to point towards the kitchen. Toni nodded in understanding. "She's not my wife. She..." He hesitated as he groped for a word. He slipped an imaginary bra strap off his ox-like shoulders and wriggled out of an imaginary pair of panties. It was grotesque and hilarious.

When I had regained control of myself I said, "Oh! You mean a strip-teaser."

Toni nodded in agreement. "That's right. She strips."

"But what is she doing...?"

"In my kitchen?" Toni interrupted. "She came in here one night last winter. She had no money. She was hungry, cold and tired." He shrugged. "I fed her and let her sleep under this counter. Now, when she has no work — when she cannot strip, she comes here. She does a little cooking. I give her food and, sometimes, a little money. Also, sometimes..." Toni displayed a surprising delicacy at times. "Sometimes she shares my bed."

My face must have betrayed me, for Toni continued quickly, "You must understand my friend. A girl in her position has to please many men — often men she does not like. Me she likes and..." He straightened up. "I am still good in bed and with this..." He pulled a can of a popular make of deodorant from beneath the counter and signalled for me to read the wording on the side. He prompted me, "And with this I am..."

I read aloud from the label, "Fragrant and enticing." I grinned and said, "You are all that boy!" And I meant it. Beauty is in the eye of the beholder and this man was beautiful — sweat-stained T-shirt and all.

Tony leaned over the counter impulsively and grabbed my lapels. I steeled myself not to draw back from the overpowering smell of garlic as he sighed, "I want to show you something that I show to nobody since I came to this country." He released his grasp and fished under his apron. He withdrew a worn, greasy wallet from which he extracted a faded photograph. He passed it over to me. "*That* is my wife. That is my beautiful Maria."

And beautiful she was. When the photograph was taken she must have been about twenty. She had fine, even features, full lips and even white teeth. A veritable halo of long, silky black hair cascaded over her shoulders. She was truly "beautiful Maria."

I handed him the photograph and said, "She is really beautiful, Toni, but I don't understand. Where is she — is she...?"

Toni sighed. "No my friend, she is not dead, but she is as lost to me as if she was."

"Has she left you for someone else?"

Toni smiled and shook his head. "Maria would not look at another man as long as I live — or afterwards. Most Americans do not understand our ways, but I think you are simpatico. Let me explain. When I marry Maria she brings with her a dowry as is the custom in my country. I want nothing from Maria. All I want is my beautiful madonna. Her dowry is a piece of ground. Her father is not rich; this ground is very small and poor. For two years I work like a mule. I try to clear it of stones but always there are more. I scrape up soil wherever I can find it; a half pail here, a half pail there. I carry it back to my land; one kilometre, two kilometres, ten kilometres — it does not matter — it is for my Maria. We have little rain, but when it comes it washes away the soil I have found.''

As he paused I said, ''And so you decided to seek your fortune here.''

He nodded. ''One night, as Maria lay in my arms...'' For a moment he put his hands before his eyes and then continued, ''Holy Mother! I can feel her now.'' He unashamedly wiped a tear from his cheek. An Italian is not afraid to show emotion. Why should he? He has no hang-ups about his masculinity as most of us have.

Toni continued, ''I say to Maria we have nothing. There is so much I want to give you but I can't even give you enough to eat. You have no clothes. You have nothing! Maria said, 'We have each other.' She cried and pleaded as women do. I wish to God that I had listened to her. But no! I had such plans. I tell her that I will send for her in six months — one year. I tell her that everybody grows rich in America. I say to her, 'Remember Pietro Antonio.' He sent for his wife and children in two years.'' Toni grinned. ''When all Pietro's children left, half the village left. He was a very virile man.''

''When I first came to America I dug ditches, carried garbage! I took any job I could get. Every dollar brought Maria nearer to me. I sent her what money I could spare and I saved — Mamma mia, how I saved! I am not Pietro Antonio you understand. It takes me five years to buy this place. Still, I am a patient man. In two or three years this will be a famous restaurant.''

Once again my face must have betrayed my thoughts.

"This dump a famous restaurant?"

Toni was not slow to sense my disbelief. "Don't forget, my friend! This area was not always like this. The empty buildings, the garbage, the muggings, the drunks. When I first came here this was a good district. I did well. In two years I had saved a thousand dollars. Soon I could send for Maria. One night some punk came in through the back door when I was busy. I did not understand banks. My money was hidden upstairs. He took it — every cent!"

Toni's muscles tightened and his eyes grew hard. His wrath was frightening. I am not a nervous type but I drew back involuntarily. His fist thudded on the counter, setting the crocks rattling. "If I could have caught that animal I would have killed him. He robbed me not only of my money but of my Maria."

He stopped, breathing heavily, chest heaving. "It was too late. Soon the good people started to leave. I made less and less money. What did I have to offer Maria? Bring her from the peace of my village to this jungle? He swept his arms around. "To this place — my *principessa*! No my friend! If I did that it would be for love of myself — not for love of Maria. I can still send her a little money and, little as it is, in our village she can live well. And what of this?" He patted his stomach; touched his bald pate and broken nose. "No! Better she should remember me as I was. The Toni she knew is dead anyway."

Some years later Toni did return to his village. I saw to all the arrangements myself.

CATERINA EDWARDS

Prima Vera *Spring*

"The doctor," Cesare would say on his way out, "told me you must get more rest," picking up his lunch box and thermos, pulling on his gloves. "Go. Sleep," his last words before he wound his scarf around the bottom half of his face and turned to the door.

And Maria would obey him. That is, she would try. She would stretch out on their bed and close her eyes. Sleep she would tell herself. Sleep. But then she would think of all the things Cesare had said the Doctor had said. Toxemia, preeclampsia, Cesare had looked the words up in the Italian-English dictionary, but they weren't there.

N.B
med.
comm.
need
to ensure
that
non-English
speakers
understand

High blood pressure. She understood that. She could feel
the blood running through her veins, pushing too hard.
Her heart beating too fast, too loud. She couldn't lie on
her front; her stomach had got too big. If she tried her
side, she had to fiddle with the pillow. She was forced to
lie on her back, her stomach protruding, forced to lie as if
already laid out. And her hand, each time, strayed to her
chest or throat. Her fingertips counting the beats. Runaway heart, and she was stuck to this miserable house, to
this small drafty room, to the coming child, to the ap-
proaching day.

If she could be home in this time of waiting. If she
could be with her sisters, her father. If she could see his
faded blue eyes, feel his large knobbled hands on her hair,
enter again his smell, lime and pipe tobacco. Home again.
Then, she would not be afraid, then.

"How can you send me away — so far? How?"

And he had pulled away from her.

"He's your husband. Your place *is with* him."

Her place. What a place. Even in the panic of those
last days before she'd left her home to come and join
Cesare, even then she had imagined it better than it was.
So this is my America, she'd thought when she first saw
the house: the paint chipped and patchy, the front stairs
cracked, the tiny front yard littered with old tires. *Mia
casetta in Canada*. None of the houses in her village were
as flimsy as this one. Nor had she imagined how confined
she'd be to the house, locked in partly by her lack of
English and her not being able to drive but mostly by the
never-ending winter. A prisoner of this cold country.
Month after month. Her very thoughts were freezing into
the shape of the rooms and the furniture. And she could
feel the fragile walls trying to hold off the snow, trying to

keep back the cold. She could feel them buffetted, weak-
ening.

The ice was pushing in at the windows, at the corners.
Reaching for her.

How could she sleep? She hauled herself onto her
side, feet on the floor, pushed up with a small grunt to a
sitting position. She was enormous; the Doctor was right
about that. Though she hadn't liked his tone when he'd
said, "Tell your wife not to eat so much spaghetti." She
had told him, told him through Cesare, that she wasn't
eating much. Couldn't. Three quarters of what went in
came right back, from the first day onwards, all eight
months. But he hadn't paid attention. Just spoke louder.
"Less spaghetti." So she didn't tell him that they, Veneti,
rarely ate the stuff.

The baby shifted, lurched. Maria, who had just got
herself into a standing position, smoothed down her dress.
That doctor could make all the accusations he wanted; she
knew.

"It's feeding off me, sucking out my bones," she'd
said, smiling to Cesare. By the time it's born, there'll be
nothing left of me." He'd looked at her then, examined
her face closely, trying to gauge the level of seriousness
behind the light tone and light expression.

He'd said something noncommittal. Then added his
usual reassurance. "Everything will be fine. We're not in
your village now. We have doctors — and a good hospital." But all evening his eyes had returned to her face. As
if he suddenly wondered who this woman he'd chosen for
a wife really was.

"So far and to a man I don't know."

"You will," her father had said, "you will know each
other."

Cesare's old, open slippers slapped on the linoleum as Maria crossed the kitchen to the living room. She could no longer wear any of her own shoes. Her feet were swollen, doughy. Sometimes they were numb or prickly, and always she had to will them to move, pull them along. Her feet that used to run up the hill to her house, that used to fly, so it seemed, over the fields to her special spot, her circle of trees.

Maria sighed as she lowered herself carefully onto the battered sofa, then arranged her feet on the arm. Cesare was right. She was getting worse. Thinking things she shouldn't think. What had Beppi said? "Think beautiful thoughts. Concentrate on what is good and sweet and the baby will flourish."

Maria stared out the window at a bare tree, grey against the white snow and sky. She must think of spring. If she could concentrate hard enough. Primavera, she could call back that first truth. The scent of new grass, *prima*, the snowdrops at the base of her trees, *vera*, the buds on the branches, fresh and green and lacey.

She could see herself, hyacinths filling her arms, a hyacinth in her hair, buoyed by the sweet perfume. And beside her, in the gentle spring night, a gentle young man speaking soft words. She was floating on the scent and the language and the touch of the breeze on her skin.

"So far. And to a man…"

Not that she would ever have put flowers in her hair. Not when anyone could see. She would have been too embarrassed. And when was there such a smooth-faced and smooth-tongued young man? Her suitors were of a rougher mold. Except for Maurizio, her godmother's son. He'd come to visit each time he was home from university. He brought flowers, sweets. It was understood. Everyone agreed it was understood. Only she hadn't acquiesced to understanding, to his languishing glances or his moist, plump fingers casual and proprietary on her arm. Even in the piazza, his hand around her shoulder or on her elbow, guiding. His words had been not so much smooth as spongy. Maria had felt she could sink into them without ever encountering a central core of meaning. "I don't understand. What do you mean?" she would say to Maurizio as they ambled on a Sunday afternoon walk. And he would smile. "Well, you wouldn't."

Cesare, he had been different from the beginning, hard-edged in his straightforwardness. "I've come back to Italy to find a wife," he'd told her father on his first visit to the house. "I had a fiancée. That is, I thought I did. But when I got home everything had changed. And I have only three weeks left." He'd come to bring news of her oldest brother, who didn't live in the same city as Cesare did but whom he knew, nevertheless. "Two hundred miles is nothing there," he said. "The space — the room — it's fantastic."

If only she'd understood then how "fantastic" it was. Of course, she hadn't been thinking at all at the time. How else could she explain it? She'd looked at this dark, quick-moving stranger in a too tight suit and hair that stood straight up like a rooster's comb, and she was dazed. He had the brightness of the sun at noon shining on the sea, hurting her eyes.

And the stranger, Cesare, watched her from across the room, and in two evenings he chose. "I was desperate. I had so little time left," he told not only her but also all the *ragazzi* one Sunday dinner. "I had to have a wife. I couldn't return without one. I would have taken anyone. Even a whore if she was willing."

131

"Thank you." She couldn't look at the others.

Cesare laughed and passed his hand roughly over her cheeks, in and out of her hair. "I'm just amazed with what I got. My own little snowdrop."

"A mountain flower indeed," Lucio added.

"Special. And as pure."

"Enough."

He'd chosen and she, well, she had found herself in the town hall, embarrassed as Cesare shouted at the official who insisted papers couldn't be done on such short notice, mesmerized as his fist pounded the shiny desk over and over. She found herself in her cousin's wedding dress, found herself repeating the hallowed words. And when Cesare was gone and she was released from the force of his choice and began to think, it was too late.

"I don't know him. He's a stranger and Canada is so far —"

"It's ever thus in marriage. You will know him. After your years together, you'll know. And you are his wife. Before God."

His wife before God. Before. The child flailed. Before.

A sudden sharp sound. She lay still, waiting, her feet still up. What else could she do? But it was only Nico, lunch-bucket in hand. She didn't like his seeing her so laid out, but to start thrashing around to get up would be worse. She'd always felt more awkward with him than with Lucio or Mario or Beppi. He rarely said much, and the paucity of words together with his stockiness and jaw-heavy face gave him a sullen, hulking presence.

"Is there any mail?" It was always his first question. Though, of course, it was the primary concern of all the *ragazzi*, no matter how politely the others might first inquire after her health.

"Not for you. There's a letter for Beppi." She started to hoist herself to a sitting position. Nico did not offer a helping hand but continued to stare down at her. A bit irritated, she said without thinking, "It has been a long time since she wrote to you. Maybe you should start worrying."

His expression didn't change. "Twenty days." He suddenly put out his hand to her.

In the kitchen she began the supper preparations. She felt even more clumsy and misshapen than usual before him. Not that Nico was watching her. Each time she turned from the counter or sink, he was staring down at his hands. He had never sat with her before. Normally he stayed in his room. He had a record player and many 78's of operatic arias. He played them for hours, *Vesti La Giubba* and *Addio Gloria* infiltrating the whole house. He did sit in the kitchen some evenings, but only when all the *ragazzi* were there. He liked to play cards and to harmonize on an impromptu song. He particularly liked to be coaxed into giving a solo. He had a good baritone voice, with only a slight tendency to shout.

"I didn't know you used cans."

Maria nearly dropped a can of chicken broth. "I don't. Only the natural, of course. Everything homemade. But now," she could feel her face flushing, "I can't stand the smell of it cooking. Makes me ill. Tomato sauce too… You do understand? You won't say anything?"

Nico murmured an "of course" and went back to staring at his hands.

What did he want? She didn't like cooking at the best of times, and being watched made it worse. Maria hadn't known how to cook when she got married. That first night she'd arrived in Edmonton, on top of her disappointment with the house, her shyness with Cesare, on top of her grief

133

at leaving home, the crowning touch was the realization she was expected to care and cook for not only one man, but five.

Cesare had noticed her expression. He immediately guided her into their bedroom and sat her down. "We can ask them to leave. It's up to you. I won't impose them on you." And when she didn't answer, "I know it's hard. I remember what it was like for me four years ago. Did I ever tell you that after the first six weeks, I made up my mind to go back? I thought cold country, cold people. It's not the place for me. I was on my way to buy the ticket." His arm crept around her shoulder. "But Mario and Beppi, they walked all the way to the ticket office with me, trying to persuade me to stay. I was at the door when what they were saying began to sink in. Friends make all the difference in this place. You'll see. Surrounded as we are by strangers — just to come home and hear the sound of our dialect." He paused and turned her head so that she faced him. "It makes me feel not so far from home." His touch on her face was assertive. "And they do pay me well. It's a way you can help. We can get back home faster."

At the end of the three days she'd asked for in which to decide, she told Cesare they could stay. It didn't take much to understand that otherwise with Cesare working at two jobs she would be almost always alone. The *ragazzi* helped keep the ice from her heart. The teasing, the laughter and the songs were insulation against the winter winds.

"We thought you were *in servizio*," Mario had said quite soon after she arrived. "We counted on it."

"I was." Maria was indignant. "But I never cooked. I was the children's nursemaid. I was in service to the Count and Countess Cicogna. I certainly wasn't expected to cook."

134

"What about at home?" From Beppi.

"My stepmother did it all. And before her my older sister... I was never interested."

"Ohho," Mario, as usual, was smiling. "And what feasts we dreamt of. When Cesare told us you were coming. Such banquets. After my days in that wretched house with only a hotplate. I thought what luck. Now — now — everything will be put right. Cesare, you should have thought of this. Given each prospective bride a test."

They'd all laughed. Except Maria. Though it didn't take her long to see that it was no use getting offended. They did, indeed, need those meals, reproducing as closely as possible what they had eaten at home.

Lucio, the one with the best profile and the big dark eyes, gave her lessons in the basics: broth, minestrone, sauce, and so on. He spoke Italian with her rather than the dialect he used with the others, and that, with his deliberate, slow movements and his formal manner, "now one measures out," gave a ritualistic tone to those lessons. The slicing, the frying, the boiling, *the* preparation of the meal.

"I've been laid off." Again Nico's words, after the long silence, startled her. He was staring at her, waiting.

"It's so cold working outside now. Maybe it's for the best. You have enough stamps for unemployment, don't you?"

"Barely enough. But, you see, the less I earn the longer until I can ask Milvia to marry me." His cheeks were flushed. "I'm tired of waiting... I need a wife."

The need for a wife, Nico, Beppi, Mario, Lucio, they all came back to that, over and over. At home, they had had mothers, aunts, sisters, friends. There were ex-schoolmates and the girls that walked the *passeggiata* in the evening. But here, except for Maria, their daily lives

135

were womanless. They ogled any girl they saw, of course; there was a convent school near the house and Mario in particular would stand beneath the dormitory windows and call up. But there was never any real contact. And they hadn't been raised to be the type of men who went to whores, not unless they were desperate. A wife, she could replace all the women each had felt he had lost. She could take care of and care for him, certainly; but more, she could save him from losing himself in this land of indifferent eyes. Woman, she could protect him from the brute state he felt he could be so easily reduced to: beast of burden, lustfilled animal.

That evening, as, with Lucio's help, she cleared the table, they began again. Beppi was smoking and complaining, complaining and smoking. Gina, his fiancee, had announced that she wouldn't come to Canada unless he promised that they stayed no longer than five years. "Ridiculous. Five years. And she expects me to sign a legal document. No trust."

"At least she writes to you. At least you have it fixed. You and Lucio are the lucky ones." Nico poured himself another glass of wine.

Mario picked three oranges from the fruit bowl still on the table. Pushing his chair back a bit, he began to juggle and hum the old song, "Scapricciatello".

"Why do I fool myself about Milvia. She doesn't write any more. It has been so long..." Nico was drawing the bottle towards him again.

Mario missed an orange. It fell, plaff. "I may have the solution for you." But he kept on with the remaining two. "Did you notice that little dark-eyed sweetie in church the last two Sundays?" He had all their attention now. "Tiny. Brown hair. And a white coat, I think."

136

"I thought she was here to marry one of the Neapolitans."

"She was. But she'd never met the groom. And when she got here and saw him, she refused to go through with it."

"I don't see how this can help me. And how do you know anyway?"

Mario was easing himself into a standing position, still juggling.

Maria began to bend over to pick up the orange. Her stomach tightened as it had many times in the last week, but this time there was an undertow of pain.

"The supposed brother-in-law-to-be works with me at the packing plant. He's indignant of course."

"But why," Beppi asked, "would she be interested in Nico?"

"So pretty," Lucio added.

"Think. She's from the South. If she went back, there would be a scandal."

"But how do I start? How do I approach her? Where's she staying?"

Mario began to dance around the table. He swiveled his hips and pretended the oranges were mariachis.

Non conosci femmene
Tu sei guaglione
Va giocare a pallone.

Her abdomen tightened again, and again there was pain. "I have to lie down."

They all focused on Maria. "Are you tired?" "Do you think it's starting?" "What's wrong. You're very pale." "Your stomach?" "It's not time yet, is it?" "I

thought the spring." "Late March Cesare said." "What is it?"

"I don't know. I don't know what it's supposed to feel like. No one told me. I don't know."

"We'll call Cesare."

"It comes and goes."

"That's it, I'm sure of it. Go and phone, Lucio."

"Some wine?"

"Breathe deeply."

Her whole body was clenching. The *ragazzi* were still asking questions, but their voices were a background roar to her. She was frozen to her chair, unable to move.

Her runaway heart was speeding, the blood pressing against the pain. If she could run away, if she could escape the pain that came not from within but without, escape the alien force that was squeezing, squeezing the baby out.

If she could get home, if she could see her father's eyes, faded and blue, if she could smell...

"So far and to a man I don't know."

Cesare was with her now, his eyes wide with emotion. 'Calm. Stay calm." He kept saying but in a sharp, loud voice. He rammed her feet into his boots, pushed her arms into his parka. He was still so unexpected, so strange to her.

"You will know him."

Papà, no, Mamma. It was her mother's eyes, those first eyes, that she needed. Though she couldn't remember them, not as they were. When she tried to conjure them, she saw the steady gaze of a black and white photograph. She could recall her presence, her arms and lap, being held in a darkened room. But that was all.

To call Mamma was to long to see again the well-tended grass in the cemetery on the hill behind the village, to long for the scent of oleanders Mamma, she had been told, planted along the front of their house. To call Mamma was to long for the primary comfort that should have been.

In the car, shivering partly with cold, Maria stared out at the dirtied streets. "What do they do with the coffins? Do they keep them stacked up somewhere?"

"What do you mean?"

She gestured at the piles of snow in the yards, glinting under the streetlights. "The land is too hard. How could they dig a hole?" She wanted to say more, much more. But she held back. Cesare was so quick to anger, and she didn't want to be called *stupida*, not again.

In fact, Cesare didn't answer her. He kept staring straight ahead. Only after the next pain, when she'd forgotten that she'd said anything, did he glance at her. "Everything will be fine. We're not in your village now. And you're not your mother." The words and the voice, a quiet voice he'd never used before, broke through to her.

For the first time, she began to cry before him. "I'm afraid."

"No need."

"I'll... I can't do it."

"Of course you can." Then, in a different tone, "Come, we're here. It's time to go in."

"Time..." Maria stared at the brightly lit emergency entrance. Cesare opened her door and extended an arm. She didn't move. He reached in and pulled at her legs.

In the last months the house and the car had both imprisoned and protected her. Now, outside containment, in the moments of unrelieved winter and in the many hours of corridors and hospital rooms, she was exposed.

139

She had already lost much that she was in leaving home. Now the nurses took away her clothes; they sent away Cesare; a small blond one unlatched her fingers from his arm. They prodded and palpitated. They gestured and jabbered. The small one flashed a long rubber hose in front of Maria's eyes. She was commanding her to do something, but what? Her pursed little mouth barked at the aide. Immediately hands were upon Maria, shoving her on her side, spreading her buttock cheeks. She had been crying silently but could no longer hold back. "Mamma," she called, "Mamma." Being helped to the toilet, being washed, being shaved, two aides holding her, one each leg. "Mamma."

"Sshhush," said the blond nurse, her freckled face scrunched in disgust. "Italians!"

Maria understood that. She wished she had the strength to sit up and punch her in her flat stomach. She did try and lift a leg. But now the nurse was talking to someone in the corner. The doctor floated into view. He was pulling on rubber gloves — inspecting. Not her face. He never looked at her face or into her eyes. He thrust his hand inside her. "Big," he said over her stomach to the nurse and then something, "spaghetti."

But the pain was blotting out the room, the doctor, and the nurse. It was tearing up time, tearing up any pause. It was tearing her apart. "Mamma." A prick on her arm, and she no longer heard her own cries. More hands. "Mamma," she was whispering. The pain was no alien force. It was her very center.

She was in another room with shiny walls. A bright light shone in her eyes. The nurses were masked. And her doc-

140

tor, — she recognized his icy eyes though. Finally, she must be close to the end. A rubber mask was handed to her. She understood "gas," a solid word in a stream of sounds.

The pain no longer possessed her. A still terror had beaten it off. A frozen sea, a still sky, icebergs. Where was this place? What was happening? She was floating in icy whiteness. There was no up or down, no signposts and no sounds. Only the relentless white. And she was falling, slowly spiralling down, ever down. She thrashed against the fall, stretching her hands to catch onto anything that might be there. Where was she? More, who was she? But her mind was as white as the featureless world. She was lost.

But, as suddenly as the fall began, her hands were no longer grasping at air. She was holding something solid. The whiteness was separating into colours and shapes. She could make out murmurs, metallic sounds. Her baby was in her arms. Perfect to see, to smell, to touch. Maria's head was still spiralling, still confused, but her boy had grounded her. Indeed, though she was not to know it for many years, his pudgy body was her first connection to the hard, foreign land. She was saved and she was bound.

GENNI DONATI GUNN

The Middle Ground

They came to live in Vancouver after her husband died: Rosalba and her small son, Claudio — her son who, in spite of her husband's persistent teachings, grew more Canadian each year. When he was born, Giulio had made her promise to speak only Italian to the boy — a rule she insisted upon even now that he was almost six. But the boy grew more Canadian each year. He would sit on her lap and listen attentively to stories (in Italian, always in Italian) about her parents. "*Il nonno e la nonna,*" Rosalba had taught him to say. But he had no grandparents here, no olive trees and no watermelons to hug. Claudio told her the other children laughed when he told them these stories. The boy had never been to Italy. His imagined homeland was no different to him than Canada had been to Rosalba before she came. It was not his fault that he could not remember the taste of prickly-pears, persimmons and fresh fruit.

In Vancouver, Rosalba bought persimmons in a little Chinese store on Commercial Drive. But they had been picked too soon and she could not find the right words to describe to Claudio their real taste.

She'd been in Canada almost ten years, had come at nineteen to live in Victoria where Giulio taught Italian Studies at the University. But Rosalba had always loved Vancouver, its mountains and ocean so close together she could almost smell the Adriatic Sea: Trieste leaning lazy against low-slung mountains, rooftops baked ruddy in the hot summers. From the viewpoint up near the Conservatory in Queen Elizabeth Park, she could almost imagine herself sitting on the stone wall of the old castle that overlooked Trieste. Only the cobblestones were missing and the long steep hills and curved narrow roads leading to the university. In Vancouver, a different beauty: the clumps of evergreens, cedar-shake roofs and coloured houses. Then the downtown high-rises jutting into the sky, dwarfed by the backdrop of mountains.

She came to Vancouver to teach Italian at a school set in Little Italy and filled with a mixture of first — and second — generation Italian teenagers. It had been the natural thing for her to do, now that Giulio was gone. Many of the students came from small villages in southern Italy and spoke only dialects. Most had never learned proper Italian grammar. Strange that she should be the one to recreate with patience a language and a culture for strangers' children — she, who could not keep her own son from becoming Canadian.

The changes had been subtle. Like the night he'd asked her to read him a story in English, although she always read to him from *Il Tesoro*. She had been raised on it herself. The thick red volume with gold-embossed printing on the cover, the fairy-tales and jokes and pictures — all part of her childhood. She could almost recite each word by heart. She'd said "no," of course, and read him his favourite story. But the next day, seized with unbearable guilt, she'd gone to a book store and bought *Peter Pan*, in English.

And another evening, when he'd asked if they could order pizza with pineapple on top, she'd said, "absolutely not, that's not real pizza," and had made him one at home, the way her mother had taught her. But later, she'd opened a can of pineapple chunks and let him put them on top of his. She was trying to keep him Italian, but the boy grew more Canadian each year.

In the area around Commercial Drive, a new Italy had been established long before she came. Here, families lived the traditional roles of their homeland. Some women were still clad in dark dresses that reached to below their knees, their elbows covered with shawls and cardigans. It made Rosalba think of Goya's *Disasters of War*. All that black — black skirts, black hair, black eyes. Only the shop windows on Commercial Drive twinkled with vibrant colours. Mannequins sporting the newest fashions from Rome smiled into the street, eyes vacant, smooth blond bobs and turned-up noses. Rosalba wished they didn't look so *American*. She'd always said *America* when she was in Italy, even though she'd been speaking of Canada. From across the ocean, there had been only one continent, no differentiation between countries. She supposed it was the same for Italy. Canadians thought of Italians as one people — all born of the same fat little dark-haired Italian Mother Earth. But she had only to think of her youth, of the many provinces and dialects, of the animosity between North and South, water and mountains.

She had chosen Vancouver, when her husband died, because of Commercial Drive, because of the mountains and the ocean. When the insurance money came, she went house-hunting with Claudio. At first, they looked in the Italian district. Rosalba tip-toed politely from house to house. "The bathroom counters are all marble. My husband had it sent direct from Italy, you know." Windows shuttered, floors glistening, Madonnas mounted on corner altars in the hall. "And that couch belonged to my grandmother. But we're going back. I'll sell it, if you're interested." Plaster busts of Roman Emperors; outdoors, lions guarding a driveway and at the back, a clothesline to the hydro pole. "These dryers make clothes yellow." And the neighbours peering from doorsteps. "And where are you from, Signora?" All so *Italian*. After the fifth house, Rosalba hurried Claudio into the car seat and drove back to their rented apartment. Inside, she took a deep breath and leaned back on the couch. She had panicked back there, among icons and idols; she felt she might be absorbed into their darkness, their familiarity. She waited a few days, then contacted a real-estate firm. She asked the school secretary to call for her. "It's my accent," she explained apologetically. "They think I'm stupid."

The real-estate lady showed her houses on the West Side, tall beautiful wooden houses made of bleached grey cedar and nicked with skylights that captured the dawn. She loved these monolithic structures, the white inner walls and the echo of her heels on the hardwood floors. Although she longed to live in one of these houses, she settled finally on a sturdy, squat bungalow with precise rectangular windows with nine panes in each. She bought it because of its cream stucco exterior that reminded her of the white stone of her parents' house. She bought it because it seemed more *Italian*, and this was her concession for not buying one within the Italian district.

She enrolled Claudio in first grade at the elementary school just two blocks away from their new home and made arrangements to have a babysitter take him there in the mornings and pick him up at the end of the day. She had to leave much earlier than he did, to drive across town and be settled into the classroom before her students arrived.

"Now don't you let anyone call you anything but *Claudio*," she said on the first morning, squeezing him to her and wishing she could go with him. "Repeat it slowly if they say it wrong." Rosalba hated the way people here pronounced her name "Rozelba" or "Ruzolba", as if there were no such thing as a soft *r* or *s*. Often, she tried to break it down phonetically: "Ross-al-ba," or "Row-sal-ba, like rosary," she'd say. But they forgot too soon.

At her school, she noticed Peppi Armano immediately. He had a physical disability and always entered her ninth grade class after all the other students were seated. He had large eyes — round white saucers with pupils swimming in the middle, which followed her around the classroom.

He walked slowly, painfully, his small hands grasping the combination locks on the lockers that lined the hallways. Her classroom was upstairs, and she grew accustomed to the shuffling of feet after the bell had rung. At times, she watched Peppi make his way up or down the stairs, one foot at a time on each step. She wanted to help him, to take his free hand, the one which was not so tightly clasped to the banister, and walk down with him, but she was afraid to show her concern because Peppi kept his head down and stared only at his feet. At the end of the first week, he stayed after class and stood in front of her desk until she prompted him, "Is there something I can do?" He blushed and for a moment let go of her desk with both hands, trying to stand up straight as he spoke. "About my being late," he said in a muffled, quiet voice, "I have to wait until the others have gone. It's easier when I can hold on to the lockers. My legs...," he stopped and leaned against the desk and Rosalba felt tears sting in her eyes. "I understand," she said. But she didn't and later, asked the Principal about it.

"Friedreich's ataxia," the Principal told her. "His parents want to buy him a wheelchair, but he won't hear of it. He's a very stubborn boy. We've talked to him on many occasions."

After that, it seemed her ears were attuned to the sound of Peppi's small feet as they dragged through the halls. She could hear lock after lock swinging on its gate after he'd passed. She imagined she could count the lockers by his steps, by his hands which clung to the round black dials. She asked the Principal if she could have a room on the bottom floor. But he said it was impossible to reroute the school for Peppi. There were too many classes, too many students, too many timetables. "We have to do what's best for the majority," he said. And Rosalba laid in bed at night and tried to think of ways to help one small boy.

She noticed that Peppi remained reserved and always

a little apart from the rest of the students. On one occasion, when she organized an after-school trip to the Italian Cultural Centre to see an Italian film, Peppi did not come. She waited for him until one of the students told her that his brother had taken him home at the usual time.

Rosalba went to see Mrs. Crombie, the school counsellor, to ask about Peppi's family.

"As far as we can tell," Mrs. Crombie said, "the parents are overprotective. The boy has no friends — in fact, goes nowhere without either one of his parents or his brother. If only he'd agree to use a wheelchair." She paused. "Has he talked to you about it?"

Rosalba shook her head.

"Poor kid. Last year, we tried talking to the parents... but you know how it is with these families. They believe they're doing what's best for him." She tapped her pen on her desk for a moment, then looked up at Rosalba. "Why don't *you* talk to them? They might listen to you, if you spoke in their language." *Their language*. Rosalba noticed the choice of words. Mrs. Crombie had not said, *your language*. *Their language*, as if *they* were somehow different from her. She said, "It's *my* language too." And Mrs. Crombie smiled. "Yes, but you're different." Strange the concept of foreigners. And how cultures could be massed under one umbrella. Yet individuals were considered separate. She wanted to shout, "I'm Italian." But she shook her head instead and said nothing. When she was still in Italy and the tourist season began, she had thought of all Americans in the same way. She had never considered each person as separate and distinct, but rather had seen Americans as a collective of brash, loud, forward peoples, with bermuda shorts and cameras. And when she'd had occasion to meet one, she too had thought that one person was

149

different. The prejudice, then, came out of ignorance, out of the stereotypes they all accepted.

"What is a Wop?" Claudio asked.

Rosalba said, "Schoolchildren often give names to things they don't understand. You are *Italian.*"

"I don't want to be Italian," Claudio said, "because Italians are Wops. And I don't want to be a Wop."

The first few weeks of school passed quickly. She was busy with marking papers, remembering names, preparing a five-minute skit in Italian to be performed for the school. I must do something about Peppi, Rosalba thought, just as soon as I'm more settled. She became aware that Claudio had started to speak English to her at home. At first, he began with a sentence here and there that she asked him to repeat in Italian, as if she couldn't understand. Two months into the school year, Claudio announced, "I'm not going to speak Italian at home any more." Rosalba pleaded with him (in Italian), "You'll forget the language," she said. Then, "If your father were alive, he'd be heartbroken." But Claudio was obstinate. "I don't want to," he said. "What's the use of it, anyway? Nobody in my school speaks Italian." And Rosalba went to bed feeling guilty and thought about what Giulio would have done in this case. Giulio would have enrolled the boy in a school in the Italian district, where he would be with other Italian children. Each day, he grew more Canadian. And she was afraid to draw him back, to make him live a life he'd never known. She noticed that her students at school were distressed, secretive, trying to cope with the mixture of cultures — their survival dependent on the separation rather than the integration of the two. Was it fair, she thought, to force them to abide by rules that made no sense here, rules which had been implemented for a different culture in a different time?

What startled her the most was that the majority of the Italians she'd met adhered to strict oppressive customs to which she had not been exposed even in Italy. They had brought with them a culture several decades old. Things changed, times changed even in Italy, but these people insisted on remaining the same. "If you stand still, you go backward." She'd read that somewhere, and now the words appeared to make much more sense.

Rosalba asked Peppi to come and see her after school.

"I'll have to phone my brother and tell him what time to pick me up."

"I'll call him," Rosalba said, "and tell him not to come."

He looked at her doubtfully. "Oh, he'll come anyway."

Peppi arrived at 4:00 p.m., after the school halls had thinned out. He stood at her desk and when she told him to sit down, he reluctantly did so. She thought that if he could have managed it, he would have run out of the room, so much did he resemble a trapped animal.

She stared at the papers on her desk and tried to find opening words. "Peppi," she finally began. "I had a talk with Mrs. Crombie."

"It's about the wheelchair, isn't it? Why does everyone talk behind my back?"

"No one is talking behind your back. We're all very concerned about you. Your parents —"

"I'm tired of their concern." His voice rose in pitch. "They always decide everything for me. Nobody asks me what I want."

She stared at him for a moment, then asked softly, "What do *you* want, then?"

"I want to — be myself," he said. "I want to do things myself. They treat me like I can't even think."

"Maybe they're trying to do what's best for you."
She paused. "If you can think for yourself, then surely you
must realize that a wheelchair would help you tremen-
dously."

"I can manage just fine on my own."

She said nothing, waiting, noting the tremor in his
words. "And besides, if I get the stupid wheelchair,
they'll never let me out of their sight. I don't want it!"

"You know," Rosalba said after a moment. "It
might not be at all how you think. With a wheelchair,
you'd be able to get around on your own a lot easier. For
instance, you wouldn't need anyone to take you to or from
school."

"Oh sure. As if they'd let me go alone." He sat,
quiet, staring at his hands. "I'm not even allowed to go to
a movie by myself. Not unless Papa drives me. It's *embar-
rassing*. Being watched all the time. If it wasn't for the law
here, I bet I wouldn't even be allowed to go to school;
they'd keep me at home always."

"Do you want me to talk to them?" she asked.

He shrugged. "I don't think it would do any good."

A few days later, Rosalba called Peppi's parents and
asked them to come to the school to speak to her. She distinctly said she wanted to see them both.

They came a little past six. She'd asked the babysitter
to stay late, even though Claudio had insisted that he was
old enough to be left alone for a few hours. Mr. Armano
was short and round and Rosalba could see that the boy's
beauty came from his mother. She was dressed much older
than her years. She could not have been much more than
thirty, yet she carried herself like an old woman. Her hair
was smoothed back into a bun at the nape of her neck,
tight and shiny, making her eyes — Peppi's eyes — appear

even larger and rounder than they were. Mrs. Armano kept wringing her hands. "Is something wrong?" Mr. Armano said in English as soon as he walked into the room. "Peppi did something bad? We teach him in the house. We give him the manners —"

"No," Rosalba interrupted, and spoke in Italian. "He's done nothing wrong. He's a very good student." The Armanos looked at her, puzzled. "Then why did you want us to come if there's nothing wrong?"

Rosalba made them sit in two of the desks of the classroom. She explained to them that Peppi was growing up, that he needed to spend time with people his own age. She asked them why Peppi had not come to see the film with the class.

Mrs. Armano clenched and unclenched her hands on her lap. "He's sick," she said.

"He has a *physical* disability," Rosalba said more sharply than she'd meant to, "but this doesn't mean he can't do a lot of things other boys his age do."

Mrs. Armano looked away. "But he might hurt himself —"

"Mrs. Armano, it's part of growing up. You know that. You've raised another boy."

"Yes, but Peppi is different," she said solemnly.

"Perhaps you're trying to keep him different," Rosalba concluded.

And that night, after she tucked Claudio into bed, she thought about the Armanos, about the fine line between protectiveness and suffocation, about Peppi's symbolic stand against it. She heard Claudio's voice a few days earlier:

"Mamma, don't hold my hand when we're out."

"But why not?"

153

"I'm too old and Jimmy says only babies hold their mother's hand."

She had told him about her family — her brothers and sisters — and how they still held hands even as adults. But he'd slipped his fingers out of hers as she talked and hooked them into the opening of his pocket. Claudio becoming more Canadian — was she, too, trying to keep him different?

She acted as mediary between Peppi and his parents, spoke to them twice more over the next month, and was finally able to convince them to agree to a compromise: they would allow Peppi to come to school alone if he used the wheelchair. It was only a small concession, but for Peppi, the first triumph of a new independence.

She watched him anxiously that first day, his hands caressing the chrome of the large new wheels. He smiled shyly at her at the end of the day, when he left her classroom with the other teens.

She sat at her desk, long after they'd all gone, and thought about Claudio and herself. She too was trying to do what was best for him. She thought of Giulio, his smile there in Trieste. He'd preserved laughter and bittersweet memories like pressed flowers of intense moments with his family and friends. He had not been rigid. He had embraced the new way of life and enriched it with the old. Rosalba remained in her classroom, thinking, until the janitor asked her to leave so he could lock up the school.

When she arrived home, she saw Claudio sitting at his little table, drawing a picture for her. "I missed you," he said in Italian and buried his face in her skirt. "I missed you too, Claudio," she answered in English. Then she took him onto her lap and told him stories of Italy.

DOMENICO D'ALESSANDRO

Wednesday Morning

Gemma feels the warmth of her hand slide down across her forehead, above the cavities of her eyes, pushing down on the nose, covering gently her lips. She notices the odour emanating from deep within the moist furrows. A maze of tiny salty streams of sweat criss-crosses the parched rough texture of her bony palm. She directs it down her neck, underneath the cotton collar, pushing a few buttons open, her fingers caressing gently her breasts. She tries in vain to remold the sagging flesh, then stops to contemplate the silent pounding of her heart. Has it really slowed down, or is it her imagining it so? She lets her left leg slide between the damp sheets, out into the stale air of the bedroom; her foot hangs down with toes barely touching the wooden floor. The sheets cling to her skin; another damp hot night has passed. She hears the refreshing hum of her neighbours' air conditioning unit, wishes she'd had one installed. It is a strain to raise her body upwards, to peel herself from the mattress. Her whole weight rests on her hips; she has to manoeuvre her shoulders to one side to compensate for balance. Both her hands join to form a bowl and rise to meet her face; with surprising vigor, they massage the sleep away from her eyes. They see themselves reflected red in the mirror in front of her, ashamed to be caught naked and completely unprepared. They search for a clue, an explanation; instead they find themselves scanning the top surface of the vanity. A metropolis of lotions and creams, brushes like miniature porcupines with their spokes raised stiffly, ready to strike a foe. Her hand takes one by the tail and brings it up to the dark mass of hair. As she strokes it, the white roots become more prominent revealing her age. She couldn't even remember the last time she had visited a hairdresser. Her fingertips trace the hairline; seems it has receded some since yesterday. She looks to the pillow for traces of lost hair to support her suspicion. Then across to the empty space, her imagination projecting the silhouette of the man that greeted her for almost forty years.

That first meeting, he stood with beret in hand, too shy to ask anyone to dance, yet continually commenting to his friends that he wasn't interested in any woman present, desperately trying to preserve the manly surface the army had tattooed on every young man.

The vigorous training made their stance rigid like those mannequins in the storefronts of the main boulevard.

Later that became a joke between the two of them, when he would comment that his stance wasn't the only thing the army had kept rigid and upright. The first time they had sex, he was very clumsy, thinking only of his own virility; it took time to come to a mutual collaboration and understanding of each other's needs. He kept asking if he was her first lover; obviously she was his first woman. She remembers whispering with some fear in her voice "yes you are," all the time avoiding his stare. That stare that hangs now centered on the right wall overlooking the bed. That same stare of innocence presiding over guilt that haunted her for years. Every time they had an argument, he'd remind her of that event and then stare at her in that fashion, knowing full well she was incapable of answering.

She had been burdened since that terrible day when the war came to an end. She ran across the bridge, down the steps, keeping her eyes scanning for any signs of his presence. She wanted to leave with him; she wanted to tell him about his child inside of her, of her love for him. The gates were closed; the SS had sealed off the northern part of the town. The Germans were retreating. Frederick was in one of the wagons bound for Milano. She clung to the gates crying until only bare trucks stretched in front of her.

Her father knocked her across the room, raising his belt to the ceiling and down across her back, screaming that he did not want a Nazi child in his house. Her brother had died a partisan, killed in a skirmish with a fascist patrol unit. This fact and her situation brought out bestiality in a man she loved deeply and thought incapable of any violence, the man who would have killed her if not for her mother's intervention. No time was wasted; the next day, arrangements were made and the following night she and her mother made their way to Carmela's house. In her

157

childhood she believed Carmela to be a witch. She remembers the woman's round face smiling at her, a soft voice
reassuring her everything would be fine. She was laid
down; her mother knelt by her side, clutching her hands.
A tall stranger came in the room followed by Carmela. The
tall woman held Gemma's legs up and apart by the knees
while Carmela poked metal tools into her womb. The pain
was piercing, her lungs exhausted from screaming. It
seemed an eternity but only a few minutes had passed. Her
whole pelvic area was in pain for days. Anna, her aunt to
whom she was sent after that ordeal, treated her very
kindly. The house was close to the sea, where she would
spend entire days, listening and looking at the rhythmical
motion of the waves. Anna was well read, had more expo-
sure to culture than her parents. She described fantastic
places she had visited, told of the people who lived there.
She gave Gemma many books to read, but for her reading
was more of a struggle than a pleasure, not having been
exposed to it before. One September day, coming back
from the beach, she saw her father standing beside her
aunt, all suitcases packed and spread around them. Without a word he motioned her to follow him. She hugged
Anna in a way to plead on her behalf, but her aunt just
stood there, sobbing quietly.

She met Joe at the local ballroom during her stay with
Anna. Her aunt loved the polkas; so every Sunday night
they would dress up and join the rest of the crowd in a
procession to the town's centre. Joe was very shy; he would
be dragged to these dances by his army buddies but never
felt at ease in them. Perhaps it was this mutual feeling of
not belonging that brought them together. When not confronted with a large crowd Joe would feel more relaxed and
be more pleasant to be with. They began meeting at the

seashore; even though she never felt the passion she had experienced with Frederick, something about Joe attracted her to him; they became good friends and would confide in each other. She missed his company back at her hometown. Her parents, greatly preoccupied in maintaining the secret, watched over her like hawks. Not being able to speak to her father, her mother lost in religious fervour, she felt all alone. Anna had never come to visit.

One afternoon her name was called from the kitchen. As she entered the room, Joe's smiling face greeted her. She wanted to hug him but the austere look of her father froze her in place. Joe had come to ask for her hand in marriage; this met with the approval of her parents, since Joe would inherit his father's butcher shop. She didn't love Joe, but this was a great opportunity to be liberated from her present situation. She knew Joe would take good care of her, and perhaps with time she would learn to love him.

The wedding day was the happiest of her life; she remembers the chaos created by the children running around the piazza. Showers of confetti hitting her skin, the very talkative photographer struggling with the people blocking his views. Antonio, her godfather, had hired a pyrotechnician to install fireworks along the path they took from the church to the house; the display was talked about for days. Her father's last hug as she entered the house. The sweet aroma of roasted almond nuts. The incredible meal which seemed never to end, and the surprise visit from Aleandro, the gypsy. He came through town on his red Fiat truck, the white player piano securely strapped to the back of the cabin, the ebony and ivory keys moving rhythmically in accordance with the scroll rolling inside. The selection of music consisted of popular folk songs and some religious hymns he would play at the patron saints' feasts of the towns he periodically visited. But the big attraction remained Curiu, the fortune-telling parrot. According to Aleandro he had dreamed one night of the Amazon and of a parrot that flew towards him. In the morning when he woke up Curiu was perched on the railing of his balcony. Once he discovered the talent of the parrot, he had the beautiful cage which he now carried around made especially for it. The cage consisted of a large centre space for Curiu to perch in and ten surrounding smaller spaces where the fortune scrolls were placed. If someone wished to know their fortune, Aleandro, after collecting the five lire he charged for the service, would open each gate; then Curiu was asked to pick a scroll. This scroll contained the future of the customer and would be given to him to read in privacy. There were those who swore on their mother's grave that the parrot had been correct in predictions on their behalf. Aleandro gave her and Joe a scroll each, but during the festivities they were lost and so their content was never revealed.

Gemma recalls the comical ordeal she and Joe went through once retired to their bedroom. Joe's army buddies had booby trapped the bed with all sorts of noise makers, so that every move they made would set off a set of bells or release some sexually-suggestive object or other. The spectacle was enjoyed by some of the guests waiting outside, below their window. The laughter grew as more mishaps began to happen; they could not help laughing themselves, and at the end of it all — the finale — a performance of the traditional bridal song — by the guests, telling in a comical vein the sexual exploits of the inexperienced.

Life in Joe's home town was pleasant for the first few years; then rumours began to spread, speculations on why they had no children. Carmela's name began to circulate among the gossip worshippers. The slamming of the door and the crashing of the glass dropped from the sudden grip Joe had on her arm told her that the secret was out. He dragged her to the bedroom and, while screaming all sorts of obscene words at her, began to tear off her clothes. She tried to run away. He forced her down onto the bed and with ferocious rage shoved his penis inside her, violently slamming his body against hers. She was panic-stricken. Joe had one hand across her mouth so that she couldn't scream. He thrusted inside of her until exhausted. His weight pinned her down; a state of pain and confusion kept her immobile. Joe began to cry; he hugged her, and for one brief moment she almost forgave him. Then he got up, dressed and left her there, all ripped and discarded, painfully trying to grasp the blankets to cover herself with. That night Joe did not come home, neither the next night, nor the one after that. She remembers vividly the stares of people as she walked the streets of the town. She dared not go home to her parents, but there was Anna. Within hours she was packed and on her way. She could smell the sea air from the cobblestone path that led to the beach; turning towards the house she noticed that the flower beds were overgrown with weeds. Something was wrong; Anna took great pride in her gardening. She dropped her bags and ran as fast as possible towards the house. A desperate cry leaped out of her as she confronted the wooden boards nailed tight to the windows and door frames. It was dark when she stood up from the old bench where she and Anna conversed for hours at a time. Defeated, she made her way back to the train station.

Joe came home after four days, entered calm and collected as if nothing had happened, sat at his usual chair in the kitchen and put a pile of papers on the table. She approached him cautiously, afraid of another violent confrontation. He asked her to be seated, said that he had sold his business and with the money they would go to America. He had a cousin in Toronto who would sponsor them. Ever since an uncle of his came to visit from Chicago, he had always had the urge to go to have a more prosperous future. He had stayed behind only for his parents' sake, but he had really always wanted to go overseas. She read right through his lie; he loved his town; he had made a good reputation for himself. He had lost face. She felt a culprit in a tragedy but in reality was the victim. Joe had already made all arrangements; she found herself bound without a choice.

It was December when they left the port of Naples on a Greek ocean liner. The cabin they were given was located below water level; they had to share it with another couple. They couldn't even sleep together; only bunk beds were provided. They could feel every slight shifting of the ship. All the cabins were packed with people emigrating to America; it seemed the whole southern Italian population was present; cries of babies, whining of children filled the evening. Everyone was complaining about the cramped quarters, not having the money to pay for the spacious cabins above. Once past Gibraltar the real agony began, for both she and Joe got seasick; the cabin began to smell worse and worse. At first the other couple complained but then they found themselves in the same predicament. The trip took a week and when they emerged on Canadian soil it was as if coming out of a catacomb. They didn't see much of Halifax, escorted on the same day from the ship to the train by a tall man in uniform who had all the information on them in a dark booklet. He motioned them to follow him to the train bound for Toronto. She remembers a white countryside with endless forests and large bodies of water frozen over. The delightful surprise at night when they passed towns; most of the houses had Christmas light decoration placed around them and the trees illuminated. She thought this was truly a great country to contain such beauty, and for the first time during the trip she began to be positive about the whole affair. Joe slept soundly beside her. She examined his face carefully and then gave way to heavy sleep herself.

Gemma looks at the clock. It's 8:30. The visiting hours at the hospital are from 11:30 — 8:00. Next to the clock there's an old photograph of Anna, squinting into the camera. It is the only photograph she had seen of her aunt and the only remaining link to her.

Once she and Joe established themselves in Toronto, she tried desperately to find out what had happened to Anna without any success. Then one day an envelope arrived with no return address. It contained that photograph and a short message:

> *Your aunt always held you in her heart up until the day she passed away. She was forbidden to see you because of her love for me. Hope you can understand. This photograph is all I can share with you.*
>
> *Patricia.*

The letter was dated almost a year before. It proved impossible to trace.

Gemma picks up the framed photo and carefully dusts the glass with her handkerchief. She wonders what

Joe would have thought if he had ever come to know about her aunt. She knows that his morals would never have allowed for this. With all the love she had for Anna, it took years before she herself could accept the situation.

The first years in Toronto proved to be a great struggle. First there was the realization that Vincenzo, Joe's cousin, exaggerated greatly when he wrote about his activities. He still had a large mortgage on his modest house; in order to meet payments he was renting all the space he could, leaving his family only the kitchen and the living room. He had reserved one room for them, but soon they had to move, for no matter how much they compromised Joe and Vincenzo could not get along. She remembers her first job, starting at 5:00 p.m. and ending at 1:00 a.m. She had to clean two floors of medical offices. Hard work was not new to her; what was unbearable were those winter nights, waiting for the bus to get home. During that time she saw very little of Joe. He worked as a labourer in a construction company; for some reason it seemed the only opportunities available to the Italian immigrant were in construction work. By the time she got home, Joe was fast asleep and when she woke Joe had been gone for hours; therefore weekends became very important. It was during these years she had begun to love Joe. They moved continuously from flat to flat, always trying to get something better and cheaper. There seemed to be a set process within the Italian community: the ones that came first would rent to others that followed; then when they had enough money they would move to a house farther away from the centre. Once boarders had saved enough, they would buy a house and rent the flats to the newcomers, until they could move to a better location and so forth. First they lived on College and Grace; then they lived near

Bloor Street and finally after five years of moving they were able to buy a house on Boone near St. Clair.

The English language was a major obstacle. She never mastered it; even now her vocabulary consists of half dialect and half English. Joe picked up more but sometimes got lost in conversation and had to revert to Italian or to an improvised form of communication. They lived in a makeshift culture, not totally Italian and not Canadian. They were in a large city, yet their world centered around the Italian section, although large, nevertheless a ghetto. There were many festivities that church organizations put on. These were desperate attempts at trying to hold on to an identity, one that kept changing faces even though the words remained the same. She remembers the first feasts and picnics, how everyone from the very old to the very young attended. It was a chance to see someone from your home town and in a subdued way a political act of strength; in numbers one felt more secure against some of the prejudices they experienced outside the community. For the young it was a chance to choose the future bride from one's country of birth. There was fear of marrying into a different culture. Now kids don't care. The young criticize most of these activities. The ghetto's walls have collapsed. There is practically no open discrimination, more prosperity and a new identity for the new generations. In spite of the struggles these were good years for her and Joe. They had become a true couple, at ease and respectful of each other.

Gemma slips into her shirt and carefully inserts the bottom edge into her skirt, so that it hangs just right. She takes one last look at herself in the mirror and then makes her way to the kitchen. In the corridor she glances up at the framed picture of St. Francis placed on the door frame, making sure that the little light bulb is still on, and quickly makes the sign of the cross as she steps underneath it. He is her favourite saint; whenever she had difficult problems to deal with, it was St. Francis she prayed to. She liked St. Joseph as well, but St. Francis seemed to be doing a better job.

Gemma reaches for the coffee maker, fills the bottom half with water and carefully measures the amount of coffee. She remembers this is what she was doing when the phone rang almost a year ago. Alfonso, the owner of the store where Joe worked, informed her that her husband had collapsed and was being taken to the hospital. As she went through two sets of doors at the emergency ward, she caught a glimpse of Joe at the end of the corridor, being wheeled into an elevator. She cried his name out loud, causing everyone to come to a standstill, while running up the corridor until she was face to face with the nurses; they recognized her to be his wife and let her into the elevator with them. During the trip up Joe didn't move. His eyes were closed; the only sign of life was the up and down movement of his chest. When the elevator opened they wheeled him through a set of green doors, and she was asked to sit in the waiting room. Hours had passed before the doctors approached her. Joe had suffered a stroke; they still didn't know how much he would recover. They kept him there for a month before entrusting him to her care. He had lost all knowledge of direction or balance; his speech had deteriorated to a muttering of a few syllables and grunts. He had lost all coordination and was practically paralyzed from the neck down. She had to feed, bathe, place him in a wheelchair and push it around. He would stare at the things he wanted and grunt softly; if he was in trouble, the sound would have a higher pitch.

Sometimes a chuckle would come out if he saw something funny.

She learned to recognize his gestures and sounds; communication became easier but only one way. She had trouble explaining to him her feelings, partly afraid to sadden him, partly out of frustration. Some nights he would grunt continuously; she felt sorry for him being denied physical pleasure. One night she happened to roll over and her breast touched his face. He grasped it with his mouth and began sucking on it ever so gently. It was a nice sensation; so she let him continue. He was completely dependent on her, like a newborn child. Ironically Joe became the child that she had always regretted not giving him, a metamorphosis in reverse to primal instincts in which raw pleasures were prominent. The immediate present was the only necessary emotion.

Joe's health worsened to the point where he no longer noticed anything around him. He had even trouble swallowing food. She had to liquify anything he put in his mouth; otherwise he could suffocate. He would defecate without warning her. Eventually she was incapable of sustaining her care for him and had to give him up to the hospital.

Gemma pours herself a cup of coffee, walks over to the door and pulls the curtains apart. The rays of the sun strike her face through the green silhouette of the cherry tree. The old wooden bench in the shade underneath, its surface cracked and furrowed, rust streaking down from the brown nails. She reminds herself to paint it sometime; she makes a mental note also to cut the grass and weed the garden. There are just too many chores for her to keep up with. She turns back into the kitchen and sits at the head of the table. Spread in front of her are the things she has to bring to Joe — a clean set of pyjamas, some shaving cream, toothpaste, some fresh strawberries and grapes that the hospital never gives him and that he loves so much. She would have to crush them first into a pasty jelly before feeding Joe. Oh yes, must not forget the ice-cream. Once a week on Wednesday she would bring him ice-cream; his eyes would light up, but he would not say anything.

A knock at the door disturbs her thought; she gets up and looks down the corridor. She hears, "Good morning, Gemma, and how are we today?" She looks at the woman, then recognizes the face; it's that nosy Beatrice, always bugging her for something or other. Perhaps today she'll go away sooner. She replies softly, "Good morning, Beatrice. I'm fine and you?" "Oh, I'm fine; that was quite a storm we had last night." Gemma does not remember a storm but she replies, "Yes, it was." "I see you're doing some cleaning up today." Beatrice motions towards the table. "No, that's the things I have to bring to Joe." Beatrice turns with a strange look on her face and with a very passionate voice responds, "Gemma, you know Joe is dead! It's almost three months now!" Gemma remains frozen. "Joe is dead?" "Yes, dear, don't you remember the funeral?"

Gemma begins recollecting a chapel filled with people silent and wearing black; then a casket. Yes, it was Joe; Joe is dead. She remembers going through Joe's belongings, the papers that he kept always locked in a briefcase. Enclosed in a brown envelope she found four letters from Anna addressed to her. The realization that Joe knew about Anna and that it was he who had kept them apart felt like a knife cutting her from within. Now she feels that sensation again. She looks at Beatrice and repeats slowly, "Joe is dead." Beatrice takes her hand, "But we could go

visit him at the cemetery for a while like we do every day.''
"Yes, that will be nice," Gemma answers. She is left in a
blank stare; her thoughts are running inside her mind,
bringing up all sorts of uncoordinated images. Beatrice
clears the table, then puts the kettle on the stove. She
looks at Gemma with a great big smile, "How about spaghetti al pesto? No one makes them better than I!" Gemma
just nods, still trying hard to make sense of everything.
Beatrice goes to her purse, takes out a small red box. She
opens it and extracts a pack of playing cards. "While we
wait, we can continue the game of *briscola* from yesterday,
remember? You were winning six to four." Gemma recalls
the games she would play with her grandfather. He taught
her how to play *briscola*; he would let her win most of the
time. She remembers the winter nights huddled in front of
the fireplace and all the stories he would recite to her and
how...

C. DINO MINNI

Changes

By three o'clock, Friday, Vitale had talked to his last client. He locked up his office early.

"Good-bye, Miss Elliott."

The girl looked up from her typewriter, squinting through large rimless glasses. "Good-bye, Mr. Di Pietro, and bon voyage."

Outside, it was snowing again, goose-feather flakes. Traffic moved sluggishly, but he had plenty of time to catch his flight. He had packed the night before. The two suitcases waited, like orphans, in the middle of the front room.

The house was empty, silent. He almost expected to find another note by the telephone. (*No point in discussing the reasons again. Jennifer.*)

He phoned Tina, his sister, to check up on his kids; they were out in the snow. She must have held the receiver up to the window, for he could hear their yelling.

Not to worry, she said.

He dialed for a taxi.

The Calgary airport was bustling, but Toronto that evening was bedlam: baggage, children, tearful relatives. There were embraces as the CP Air flight was announced. Half the city's Italians, it seemed, were going back for Christmas.

By three o'clock, Monday, he was on the train to Rome. He had decided not to spend time in Milan after all; the city had few memories for him. He'd been there scarcely one year, the ink still wet on his lawyer's diploma, before Canada and family ties had lured him away.

It was drizzling and cold when he came out of Rome's Stazione Termini. His first thought was to take a horse cab to Piazza Trilussa, but he saw none. Probably none left. There were several Fiat cabs parked under the street lamps. The driver of one solicited him as he stood in the rain, undecided.

"*Tassì?*"

Vitale ran for it. The driver threw his suitcases into the back and flipped the meter lever to "on". He was a paunchy man, his hat askew, a cigarette hanging from his lips. A typical Roman cabbie, grouchy at the world.

He was taking a roundabout way to their destination to increase his fare, but Vitale didn't mind the tour: that's what he had come for. (*A rest, the doctor said. A change of scene.*) He leaned back. In the streets ahead traffic snarled, and the coloured lights of shops spilled and splashed onto the wet pavement. But he had only to close his eyes to hear the clip-clop of a horse cab on the deserted cobbles, past the ghostly marbles of the Forum. A girl beside him.

(*You left someone back there, didn't you?*)

The driver swore at a pedestrian. They were passing the Colosseum and headed towards the Sant'Angelo bridge. Vitale looked up at the archangel over the circular fortress that had once been Hadrian's tomb and was almost relieved to see it there, in the moonlight. He thought of Puccini's Tosca throwing herself into the Tiber. As a student he had been an avid opera fan, when he could afford the tickets.

By the time they reached Piazza Trilussa, in the Trastevere district, the rain had stopped. The driver let him off by the fountain. It was, as he remembered, like a rectangular picture frame set on end at the top of a low dais. In summer water poured from a high font and splashed into a basin below; now it was frozen.

As the taxi drove off, he looked for other remembered landmarks. The statue of the poet Trilussa still leaned on one elbow. Beyond the square was a walled sidewalk along the river, where he saw the student walking; above, the skyline was crowded with belltowers and cupolas.

He picked up his suitcases and walked the rest of the way to the pensione. Twenty-three years, but he recognized the owner; he was the same small, bald man, his remaining hair gone completely white.

Vitale asked for Room 11, if possible.

The owner (Vitale remembered his name now, Carlo, and the wife's, Luisa) seemed surprised. *Certo*, certainly. It was the off season. He could have almost any room.

"How long would the signore be staying?"

"A few days." Vitale signed the register with his gold-plated fountain pen, asked after the Signora Luisa.

The owner peered over his glasses at this *americano* in a cowboy hat. Vitale explained that he had roomed there as a student at the university before emigrating.

"Ah, *si*." The old man rummaged in the attic of his memory. "I seem to remember..." But he didn't, probably had him confused with someone else. Luisa, he said, was dead these three years.

He took a key and came around to help him with his suitcases.

Entering his room was a step into the past. The same Venetian blinds, flowered wallpaper, cracked mirror. The same Modigliani print on the wall. He opened the bathroom door, and, yes, found the student, soaking in the tub. The hot water relaxed him; it made him drowsy.

The knock on the door startled him — "Is anyone home?" And a woman's teasing laugh, clear and high-pitched. Luisa.

Dead, these three years.

"*Scusa*," the owner apologized, looking at the towel around his midriff, the wet footprints on the ceramic floor. "*Scusa*, your receipt."

Vitale dressed again and went out, looking for the small trattoria with paper tablecloths and sawdust on the floor. The student always ate there, settling his account at the end of the month. *O Cavalluccio*. A white stallion pranced above the big spiked double doors, three steps down from the pavement.

Inside, the sawdust was gone and tables had linen cloths. He looked up. The rafters were gone, covered by a new ceiling, from which pointed chandeliers like imitation

174

lanterns hung above the tables and cast a yellow light. But the clientele was the same, mostly families from the neighbourhood.

The proprietor put a flask of white Frascati in front of the law student, and took his order: *il piatto caldo*, the cheap hot pasta dish. (He was only a postman's son and had to be careful with his meagre allowance.)

The order arrived, hot *gnocchi* with meat balls, and the proprietor spread a napkin to protect the customer's shirt from the rich sauce.

He ate ravenously, having had nothing but a sandwich on the train. Where was the guitar player who used to go from table to table, singing ballads for the price of a meal?

He wore a red sash from which hung a tin cup. Strangers were his best patrons, and he had already spotted the blond girl with the young law student. It was the first time he had brought her there.

"*La biondina?*"

She gave her name, Elvira, and Vitale threw a coin into the cup.

The man strummed his guitar, found the right key and burst into a somewhat bawdy song about a girl named Elvira and unrequited love. Vitale had heard it before. The lyric was always the same; only the name of the girl changed. It never failed to produce smiles around the room, however.

That night he dreamed. He was riding in a horse cab with a girl — Elvira? Jennifer? He couldn't be sure in the dark. She was angry. They had been fighting again.

"Is it something I've done?"

"No," she whispered, face averted. She did not want entanglements. "Try to understand."

He didn't.

Instead he took the job in Milan to forget, and then in Calgary, farther away.

Vitale lay awake a long time, thinking of Jennifer — all the times she had called him too conservative, a fascist. (*I've changed, he pleaded. Changed? — with a laugh he didn't like. Only on the outside!*) He had tried to understand; really had; couldn't; then would lose his temper.

He was out early, sipped a coffee in a bar, then took a taxi to the university. It was deserted for the holiday. He walked most of the morning around the campus — a thin student with a green scarf, shoulders hunched against the cold. The air was invigorating; it cleared his head.

He paused under the leafless trees, blew on his hands, then turned for the law library. It was open. He went in, and found Elvira at a table, surrounded by books.

He sat and just watched her: elbow poised on the table, the head inclined long-lashed to the page, left hand absently sweeping back her blond hair, which she wore long, over her thin blue shoulder. She loved the law with a passion, she said.

What was she now, Vitale wondered? A judge?

One of the sacrifices of the move to Canada was his career. He'd gone into real easte, made money, but —. He shrugged. He'd done it for his family, of course. Jennifer had never denied that he had been good to her. (*But only with things!*) He wanted to reply that Canada had been good to him, also, but only with things.

In the end, however, she had asked just for her car, her potted plants and some money. He thought of her living with that man, that yuppie.

The librarian was staring at him. He became conscious, suddenly, of his attire: cowboy hat and high-heeled boots. Could she help him? No, no, he was just leaving.

He took another taxi to Piazza Garibaldi. The aroma of chestnuts roasting was pungent on the wintry air, and he stopped at a booth and bought a bagful before crossing the square to where Elvira waited in the warm purple shadows. The summer day had cooled, and they linked arms for their evening walk.

At the edge of the square was a red wooden puppet box on stilts. They watched Pulcinella and his friends and enemies bashing each other to pieces with clubs. But Elvira liked looking at the children better; so they went around to the back of the box and watched the rapt faces, mirroring everything that was happening on the noisy stage.

He was due in Villa on Thursday.

He took the first afternoon bus and settled to read a newspaper. The Roman *campagna* did not much interest him — Tivoli, Cassino; the student had made the trip many times. Across the aisle from him sat two fat women bundled in overcoats. One had a raffia bag on her lap, a veritable cornucopia from which she drew mandarins, biscuits and candy to bribe her two small boys on the seat behind.

The bus climbed higher into the Apennines, the driver leaning on his born at every hairpin curve. It stopped to let a flock of sheep cross the road. The landscape was bleak: grey fields, leafless trees, smoke from farm chimneys. Grey stone villages, and in the distance the snow-covered peaks of La Majella (height: 2 797 meters, the mountains here as rugged as the Alps.)

The driver leaned on his horn again. A man on a donkey drew aside to let them pass, wind snapping at his clothes.

He must have dozed over his newspaper, for the bus

was over the watershed now and was descending. It began to rain, flat drops on his windshield. He waited for the first glimpse of Villa, like a black-and-white postcard: stone towers and ramparts against a metallic sky.

The bus continued to descend towards the river, and then climb again, through olive groves, over a stone bridge, past the tiny cemetery with its twin pines, and into town.

It was already dusk. Street lights blinked on. The station was by the post office. A small crowd had collected to meet the bus. As he waited for his suitcases, hat under one arm, someone asked if he was the telephone inspector; they were waiting for the telephone inspector.

He walked into the post office. A blind man sold lottery tickets from a booth. Men in galoshes smoked or argued politics. A radio blared.

His father was at one of the wickets, a tall, spare man in a faded brown jacket, white mustache and eyeshield. They embraced. It attracted attention. He was recognized, surrounded. Someone pumped his arm: Luigino, Villa's soccer champion. Did he know —? Of course, they'd gone to school together. They laughed that he'd been mistaken for the inspector. In that *cappellaccio*, hat!

They walked home together, he and his father, and he described his trip and gave news of the rest of the family. (All of them well. They send their love.) His heels caught on the cobblestones, and he stumbled. His father offered to take one of the suitcases: no, no, he'd manage.

His mother came from the kitchen when she heard voices, drying her hands on her apron, face flushed from the stove. She was baking. An aroma of vanilla and liqueurs filled the house. She embraced him. How was he? And then still the mother: was he hungry? She sliced a thick piece of panettone while his father fetched up a decanter of wine, fresh from the keg. As if he were a boy again, home from school.

They knew he would be coming alone and did not ask about Jennifer and the children. He was grateful for that, as he sat there happily watching his mother bake.

After dinner, the house filled with relatives and neighbours. His father brought up another decanter of wine, and they drank, gossiped and joked into the night.

He was tired when he went up to bed but content. He fell, for once, into a dreamless sleep.

He woke to the cries of a vendor in the street below. Morning. He threw back the heavy quilt and went to the window. Through the slats in the wooden *persiane*, shutters, he could see the street. A fierce wind rattled a tin can along the cobbles, and a few old women in thick black shawls were on the way to church, shoulders bent against the cold.

He showered, then plugged in his electric razor. His eyes met, like strangers, in the mirror as he combed his still luxuriant shock of black hair. In school, he'd been called Vitalis. Later, when he told Jennifer, she thought the story was funny.

Dressed, he went down for breakfast, pausing on the stairs when he heard voices.

Esaurimento nervoso, nervous breakdown. *Ma il perchè?* The reason? And his mother's angry retort: What kind of woman leaves her children?

They changed subject when he entered. His mother had prepared hot bread rolls with orange jam and tiny cups of espresso. It was snowing on the mountains all around them, his father said, and rubbed his hands together.

179

After breakfast he went out. He wandered towards the Heights above the town, the oldest part. He passed through the Gate, all that remained of Villa's walls, and entered the Middle Ages. The tortuous streets narrowed and climbed in steps, but cobbles had been replaced like missing teeth, and the centuries sandblasted from the rough stone exteriors of houses. He looked up, at new wooden shutters and iron balcony railings painted green or red or blue.

He no longer knew these streets, and they did not seem to know him.

What was he looking for?

Half way up, he reached a small square with an arcade of shops. They were closed, but he saw in the windows clocks and boots, souvenirs and postcards, fruit and cheeses. At the far end, where a street descended from the castle, was Cafe Villa. An ancient vine grew from the dirt floor and, in summer, spread a canopy of cool foliage over the outdoor tables. The student sat in the shade, sipped iced coffee and watched village girls fetching water from the public fountain at the center of the square, copper urns expertly balanced on their heads, gay-coloured dresses blown by the wind.

The cafe was closed. He stopped only a minute there, sitting at a table on the concrete floor below a plastic covering. He looked at the fountain. The water was turned off.

Above him was the ruin of the castle. He was surprised to find an iron picket fence around it and surprised that the gate was secured with a padlock. A sign advertised the times of tours. From April to October only.

But, as in a dream, he was through the gate — a 12-year-old running through the courtyard in games of tag or war, or searching for secret passageways and hidden treasure.

Somehow these memories had become more precious as he grew older.

(*Changed? Only on the outside!*)

He turned right, following a street from the parapet of which he could look down on the roofs of the town, smoke billowing from chimneys, and farther along found the Shortcut, a steep flight of stairs carved into the granite of the mountain, which brought him down.

His mother had prepared a heavy afternoon meal, and the three of them lingered at the table companionably until his father glanced at his wristwatch and stood up; he was due at the post office.

Vitale fetched his overcoat too. He strolled down to the main piazza. The afternoon was already dark enough for the streetlights to blink on. In a gift shop, he bought a Pulcinella toy, the clown dressed in a green court jester's outfit and mounted on wheels so that it clapped a pair of cymbals as it moved. For his son. And a doll dressed in a traditional peasant costume for his daughter. He had these wrapped and packed to mail but, crossing the square to the post office, changed his mind: he'd bring them back himself.

The piazza was crowded, despite the bitter cold. Shops were still open — the baker stoking his brick oven, the barber singing softly to the clip of scissors, the cobbler hunched over a shoe, mouth full of tacks. Vitale passed a wine-and-oil shop, its floor heaped with raffia-covered flasks and giving off the odour of grape and must and wood.

To warm himself, he entered the coffee bar. The counter was crammed with pastry and sandwiches and glasses and bottles of liquor and the hot gleaming, hissing espresso machine.

(*Why do they call it expresso? Jennifer asked.*)

It was their first date.

(*Because it looks like a locomotive.*)

The barman, in a white apron, was master of this contraption, which he played like a bellows organ. The student had watched with fascination as the barman hauled each lever down at the right second all the while bantering with customers, clattering new cups and saucers and spoons onto the counter, filling the cups with a flourish and handing out sandwiches held in a paper napkin by thumb and forefinger.

Vitale sat on a stool, sipped his coffee slowly and listened to the animated conversation around him, which to his Canadian ears sounded like fighting.

Outside, it was snowing.

On the way home, gift parcel under his arm, he heard the *zampognari* even before he turned the corner. He came upon a scene like an antique greeting card: the pipers playing carols in the yellow puddle of a streetlamp, snow falling. A crowd had gathered around them, and people stood in doorways and at windows.

Each Christmas the pipers left their herds on the lonely, windy hills of Abruzzi and came down into the streets of towns. They were dressed in traditional shepherd costumes: short black capes, vests and leggings of sheepskin, and rawhide shoes with thongs around the legs and curled-up, pointed toes. They travelled in twos. One played a *zampogna* or kind of primitive bagpipe; the other a reed instrument like an oboe.

They held out their hats for tips, picked up coins thrown from windows, then moved on, followed by children.

Farther up the street they made another stop, and the scene repeated itself.

His parents' house was full of family and friends. His mother had set up a side table with hors d'oeuvres, bread rolls and wine bottles. Carols played from the stereo. He played the polite host, opening bottles, pouring wine, making himself useful with a towel on his shoulder. He was given small parcels to take back to mutual friends in Calgary. The slowness of the mails, you know. But why was he leaving so soon? In three days? He had just arrived.

Tired of explaining the reasons — his kids, his office, the difficulty of getting flight reservations around New Year — he was glad to escape to Midnight Mass. It was, he reflected, his first time in a church in years. At some point he had stopped going: too busy buying, selling, winning.

When he returned, the house was silent. In the kitchen embers still glowed in the fireplace. Bottles were empty, dishes stacked. He tiptoed upstairs. Yes, that had been the important thing, winning. He lay in bed and counted his assets: two hotels, one paid for; a ski lodge, 453 acres of land, a half share in a movie theatre, a pub, and a fine restaurant.

He was back in Calgary for the New Year. The invitation to the party was among the pile of letters, cards and flyers inside his door.

He went.

The guests were his usual friends — accountants, agents, builders. The conversation ranged from business to sports to politics. It got louder as the liquor flowed.

A woman said something about Reagan's Star Wars Project. He recognized her vaguely, replied politely.

He was passed another scotch.

How was his holiday?

It seemed, now, as if he had never been away.

"Five minutes," someone called.

"Four!"

Andy Williams was on TV from Times Square.

They began the countdown.

Outside, horns and rattling pots.

She kissed him. There was liquor on her breath.

He left early.

Drunk, he made his way back to his car. He had parked on the road at the side of the house, and across the driveway the subdivision ended in empty fields and, beyond, the prairie. He stumbled on the snowbank.

Something moved ahead of him. A small animal? He raised himself on one knee and reached out to grab it, but it moved away. He chased it, but whenever he got close, it jumped away from him.

He flailed his arms, stumbled, fell in the knee-deep snow.

He was unsure what it was, as it escaped across the prairie, or even if it had been there at all.

LISA CARDUCCI

Antonio

He is seventy-two years old, Antonio. It was when I saw that he held his newspaper upside down that I became interested in him.

"If you think about it, you make believe you're read-ing. Because in this country no one has the right to do nothing. Think about it, to sit alone on the terrace of a cafe recalling the past is only good for fools. So I pretend to read the newspaper. But you, ha! you saw through it, you trapped me."

"What were you thinking of, Antonio, when I arrived?"

"About injustice! Wait, I am going to tell you to unburden my soul.

"We had just arrived in Canada, my parents and the six kids who were born in Italy, when I began school. Eventually there were five other kids. We lived in a French neighbourhood near the Jean-Talon market. In fact this neighbourhood was full of Italians, Lebanese, Syrians, but we were only poor immigrants, which doesn't matter. We lived among francophones; I learned French quickly and finished my first year of school hands down.

"My parents, they never spoke anything but Italian. We called it the *campovasciano* language, because my father came from Ripabottoni and my mother from Provvidenti. I'd love to go there, in the meantime..."

"In the meantime what?"

"Let's get back to our sheep. So, September came and I began my second year of school. We learned English as well as French. Our teacher was a religious brother, for all the subjects. The second last day of class before Christmas vacation, he told us, 'Bring home your books, if you have any free time you can read and do math so that you won't forget what you learned.'"

"And then?"

"All the kids brought home their books, but none had any intention of studying, I thought. Me, during the holiday I got bored. There was no question of going to play with my friends; my parents were very strict on that subject. I never left the house except to go look for embroidery thread. My big sister, the oldest, Marianina, was going to get married as soon as she finished her trousseau. I never understood how she could use so much thread. So, other than two runs to the fabric store, I had nothing to do except reading exercises and math. It doesn't count that I

186

didn't mind doing it. Yes, I loved to learn. It was not a sacrifice for me to have only my books as entertainment.''

"Is that all?''

"Of course not. I haven't told you anything yet.''

"So tell me, I'm intrigued.''

"Well. When we returned to school after the feast of the Three Kings — at that time the holiday was longer than it is now — so when we returned the brother asked us, 'Who did some exercises during the holidays?' The whole class burst out laughing because the brother himself asked the question ironically. There was only another boy and me who had done some work. André, my companion, had done some multiplication. Me, I was too shy to say it, but the brother came to see my notebooks himself: the whole chapter of multiplication. In addition I had read almost the whole reader and I had written a summary. 'That merits a reward!' said the brother.

"I didn't believe my eyes: a lovely picture of baby Jesus with a gold border. I turned red with pleasure when all of a sudden from the back of the class I heard, 'That's not fair! He is Italian!'''

"For three seconds, I saw myself beside the brother who was coming to my defence. I thought that he was going to explain that he was rewarding effort and not the red, white and green flag. But no! he also lined up on the side of racism, he took the picture out of my hands and gave it to André. It was because Italians are hard workers by nature, I did not deserve a reward, right?''

Old Antonio shook his head, his bitterness awakened by this memory.

"It is hard for me to believe... and so how did you manage?''

"That day I quit school, absolutely.''

"Your parents, did they agree?"

"They knew nothing about it. Each morning, I would leave with my books. I would play in the ditches, steal some fruit in the market. I would play all day and then return home punctually at 4:30. It was months before they learned about it."

"Did they get a call from the school?"

"No, no. At first we did not have a phone. Then I thought that the school would not bother about my absence. They would think that my parents took me out of school, that's all. No, it was my sister, Concetta, who went to the butcher one day to buy some pork chops — at that time they cost 25 cents for three pounds — saw me. What a long story at home! But I refused to return to school. School was only for Canadians, at least in my little head at that time. I had decided to leave it to them."

"I understand now why you hold your newspaper upside down!"

"Not exactly, it is all an act, simple distraction. I know how to read! And I bet you that I have read more in my life than my classmates who finished school. I am self-taught. I read and write in all three languages."

"What did you do in your youth after you did not return to school?"

"I began to work at nine years of age. Delivery-boy for groceries. By law I had to be fourteen in order to work, but I was big for my age, and they pretended to believe that I was old enough. Grocery delivery-boy. At first I earned $4.50 a week.

"One day my father went to see the boss and told him: 'Listen, if you want my son you have to give him $5 a week.'"

"Was the boss Italian?"

"No, my father did not speak French, but made himself understood. The boss agreed. And I felt a little avenged over the injustice of the brother, this time the work of the brother was well repaid. In fact the boss payed only the difference between my tips and the 5$ required by my father."

"Have you gone back to Italy anytime?"

"No... no. I'm sorry to say it. It is my dream, but I have not realized it. You see, I had to help the family, then my sisters got married one after the other, and my father died. I also got married. Two of my brothers and my youngest sister remained home with my mother."

"Are you the second or third oldest in your family?"

"I am in the middle. The youngest of those born in Italy. Of eleven children, four died at a young age, between a few months and seventeen years old. In those days pneumonia took many victims..."

"It's true that they did not know about antibiotics!"

"No; nor did they have a vaccine against economic crisis or against war. One misfortune followed another. We were never able to get out of the hole, and I was never able to go to Italy," said Antonio sadly.

"Me, I was lucky enough to go to Italy two times, and soon I will be going back on business. Well, the next time I will take you with me."

Antonio looked at me tender-heartedly. We were silent and then he talked again.

"Look, now I am too old. I don't want to go anymore. I belong here, and I'm... I think I'm afraid to be in Italy."

"Why? It's such a beautiful country!"

"Things have changed there..."

"But no, I assure you! It's a country that is very..."

Antonio slowly shook his head from side to side.

"You don't understand. I don't say that Italy is not beautiful anymore, only that it is not as I knew it. I lived there only a short time but I have kept the image that my parents gave me of Italy. All my life I have felt surprise after surprise when my cousins or my friends, or some *paesani* have told me what they saw in Italy. Well, for example, my daughter. In '67 she went there on her honeymoon. Well, in the village of her husband, each family had a television, a refrigerator, even an automatic washer."

"That's good! Do you see something wrong with that?"

"No, it's not wrong, certainly not. It may be surprising... and possibly also disappointing."

"Do you mean that it is the old, folksy Italy that you want to find there?"

"Well then, now you understand. If for example, I were to go to Germany or to France I would expect to experience what they call culture shock, but Italy is my native country, where I was born and it would hurt me to see it changed. Let's take your mother. Suppose that you were separated from your mother since you were a baby, and that thirty or forty years later you were to meet her again. You would know in your head that she would have aged, but in your heart she has not changed. So when you see her again before you, maybe more beautiful than before, well-groomed, dressed in style, smiling, you may not be able to take it..."

"And I would begin to cry as if she had betrayed me."

"Just so!"

I understood. I now understood why old Antonio

would die in Canada without ever seeing his native Italy again. I understood what he was thinking about when I saw him holding his newspaper upside down as pretext. I understood that each time that I would return to Italy I would take with me the point of view of Antonio.

Translated from the French by Joseph Pivato

Biographical Notes

DOMENICO D'ALESSANDRO was born in Collarmele, Italy, in 1955. In 1978 he received a diploma from the Academy of Fine Arts of Florence, and in 1981 he graduated from the University of Ottawa with a B.A. in visual arts. "Wednesday Morning" is his first published story.

ALEXANDRE L. AMPRIMOZ was born in Rome in 1948. In 1978 he received a Ph.D. in French Language and Literature from the University of Western Ontario and is currently a full professor at Brock University. He has published 27 books and a large number of scholarly papers, critical articles and translations. A few of his most recent books include *In Rome, Fragments of Dreams, Sur le damier des tombes, For A Warmer Country* and *Bouquet de signes.*

WILLIAM ANSELMI, born in Nettuno, Italy, in 1958, is currently enrolled in a Ph.D. program in Comparative Literature at the University of Montreal. He has published in *Vice-Versa.* "The Joke of Eternal Returns" is his first published short story.

JOHN BENSON, who immigrated to Canada 20 years ago, has engaged in a variety of occupations: optometrist, antique dealer, university administrator, fencing master and more recently, author. He has published a number of articles and short stories and his war memoirs *Birds Don't Fly at Night*. Several of his short stories have been broadcast by the B.B.C. in England. He is at present working on a humorous novel about Napoleon's stay on the Island of Elba.

FIORELLA DE LUCA CALCE was born in Quebec, of parents who emigrated from Caserta, Italy. She is currently working as a secretary at Vanier College and writing and sketching in her spare time. "Pomegranate Blossoms" is her first published piece.

LISA CARDUCCI was born in Montreal in 1943. She graduated with a B.Ed. from the University of Montreal in 1963. She is fluent in five languages — English, French, Italian, Spanish and mandarin Chinese — and currently teaches French at the high school level. She has contributed to various literary journals, both as writer and as artist. Her publications include *Nouvelles en couleurs* and *Les Heliotropes*.

CATERINA EDWARDS was born in England to an English father and an Italian mother, but was raised in Alberta. She has published one novel, *The Lion's Mouth*, and many short stories in literary magazines and anthologies such as *More Stories From Western Canada*, *The Story So Far 5* and *Double Bond*. She has also written a play, *Terra Straniera*, which was produced professionally in 1986. She lives in Edmonton with her husband and two daughters.

MARISA DE FRANCESCHI was born in Udine, Italy, in 1946, and came to Canada at the age of two. In 1968 she graduated from the University of Windsor with a B.A. in English and French and is presently teaching French for The Windsor Roman Catholic Separate School Board and operates a small publishing house, Mardan Publishing. Two of her short stories have been published in *The Canadian Author & Bookman* and were subsequently included in the anthology *Pure Fiction*, edited by Geoff Hancock in 1986.

GENNI DONATI GUNN has a M.F.A. from the University of British Columbia. She was born in Trieste, Italy, in 1949 and came to Canada at the age of ten. At present she lives in White Rock, B.C., and is a Sessional Instructor in the Department of Creative Writing at U.B.C. She has published poems, fiction and translations in a number of literary magazines, including *Fiddlehead, Pierian Spring, Poetry Canada Review, West Coast Review* and *Womansong*. She has completed a translation of Dacia Maraini's poems *Devour Me Too*, which was published in 1987 by Guernica Editions, and has three new books in progress: a novel titled *Countdown*, a collection of short stories and a translation of Dacia Maraini's novel *Storia di Piera*.

DORINA MICHELUTTI was born in Friuli, Italy, in 1952, and immigrated to Canada in 1958. She studied at the University of Florence and at the University of Toronto. Her work has appeared in various magazines, and she has published *Loyalty to the Hunt* (Guernica, 1986), a book of poetry.

C. DINO MINNI was born in Bagnoli del Trigno, province of Isernia, Italy, in 1942, and came to Canada at the age of nine. He grew up in British Columbia. His short stories, articles and author interviews have been published in various literary magazines, anthologies and CanLit textbooks. From 1977 to 1980 he was a literary critic on the staff of *The Canadian Author & Bookman*. He reviewed for *The Vancouver Sun* on a regular basis for eight years, until 1984. His first collection of short stories *Other Selves* was published by Guernica Editions in 1985. He is currently editing (with Anna Foschi) the proceedings of the First National Conference on Italian-Canadian Writing, which took place at the Italian Cultural Centre in Vancouver September 15-19, 1986.

NINO P. RICCI was born in southwestern Ontario, to parents who come from Molise, Italy. He completed his undergraduate studies at York University in Toronto and then spent two years teaching English language and literature in Nigeria. He has travelled extensively in Africa and in Europe and has returned three times to the country of his parents' birth. He is currently completing a Master's in Creative Writing at Concordia University in Montreal and is working on a novel called *Rita*, portions of which have been read on the radio program *Montreal Writers on Tape*. His story "Still Life" appeared in the Winter 85 issue of *The Fiddlehead*.

SANTE A. VISELLI was born in Strangolagalli, province of Frosinone, Italy, in 1949. He has a doctorate from the University Paul Valery and is currently Assistant Professor of French at the University of Winnipeg. He has published 29 scholarly essays (some of them in collaboration with

Alexandre Amprimoz). *"Ed io anche son pittore"* is his
first published short story.

LILIANE WELCH was born in Luxembourg in 1937, where
she also completed her early education. She received a
B.A. and an M.A. from the University of Montana and
took a Ph.D. in French Literature from Pennsylvania State
University in 1964. In 1967 she settled in Canada, where
she teaches modern and contemporary French poetry at
Mount Allison University in Sackville, New Brunswick.
She has published eight books of poetry, including *From
Songs of the Artisans* and *Manstorna: Life in the Mountains* and has co-authored with her husband two books of
literary criticism on contemporary French poetry. Welch
returns to Europe each summer to study in the North and
to go mountain-climbing in the Alps.

Printed by the workers
of Editions Marquis, Montmagny, Qc
in May 1989